Biography

Terry Scales was born in 1932 and grew up in the riverside community of Rotherhithe, South London. His family were well established in the local fraternity of dockers, stevedores and lightermen and the shores of the Thames became his natural boyhood playground.

Evacuated to Devon during the war, he returned to live in one of the first Prefab villages, an experience he describes as 'a stimulating culture shock between country and city lifestyles'. The resulting contrasts left an indelible set of impressions, many of which are narrated here.

Deserting the traditional family livelihood on the river, he entered Camberwell School of Art as a Junior in 1946 and soon decided to become a landscape painter.

After passing his Diploma and serving two years in the RAF he then took the most unusual step of returning to work on the Bermondsey waterfront for five years before being summoned to teach drawing at Camberwell School of Art, a post which he held with distinction for thirty years.

Now living in Greenwich, his paintings have been widely collected and exhibited continuously in major public and private galleries.

Commissions have included the National Maritime Museum, Tate & Lyle and Scruttons PLC. The popularity of his Thames landscapes resulted in a feature interview in the Channel 1 TV film, 'The River', broadcast in December 1996. Concurrently, he publishes many articles in magazines and periodicals and continues to paint his favourite subjects on the banks of the Thames.

References

References in 'Dictionary of British Art, Vol. 6', Frances Spalding.
'Camberwell School of Art, Its Students and Teachers', Geoff Hassell.
'The Dictionary of Artists in Britain since 1945', David Buckman.

BERMONDSEY BOYS

TERRY SCALES

BLUE ANCHOR PRESS
In association with
Aspen Creative Resources Limited

III

First published in United Kingdom in 1999 in association with
Aspen Creative Resources Limited - Telephone: 01482 865345.

Blue Anchor Press
12 Prior Street, Greenwich, London SE10 8SF.
0181 853 3730

The lines from Four Quartets, Collected Poems 1909-1962 by T.S. Eliot
by kind permission of Faber and Faber Limited, Publishers.

British Library Cataloguing in Publication Data
ISBN 0 9535478 0 9

To Cristiana Angelini

...and those unsung heroes, the designers of the Prefab.

There is no end but addition.
History is a pattern of timeless moments.
T.S. Eliot.

Contents

Original Illustrations by the Author

VIII

Preface

On my infrequent trips to the market close by my old locality I had often noticed the nameplate 'Ambrose Street' attached to the flank wall of a corner shop. It was the only tangible evidence that such a place had ever existed.

Long gone were the neat terraces of artisan cottages on the left and the Prefabs stretching to infinity on the right. No trace either of the pavements lined with pollarded trees that flowed so naturally into the market where decades earlier I had worked on the sheet music stall and was sent by my green-fingered mother to sell parsley. Though much reduced in number and removed from the busy main road, the stalls had managed to survive.

Then, stopping off one day to buy fish, I noticed an empty space where the sign had previously hung. The last tiny clue had been removed. Nothing now remained to remind me of that brave new Prefab world of the post-war period. I believe that this small severing of the familiar triggered off the impulse to put down on paper my happy memories of the South Bermondsey of fifty years ago.

A week after completing my last story, I had occasion to revisit the market and, old habits dying hard, glanced up at the flank wall. To my delight the sign had miraculously reappeared to occupy its rightful place ten feet above pavement level. What combination of circumstances had resulted in the return of a sign for a street which no longer exists is an enigma.

It is right that it should remain so.

T.S.

Scuffle at the Fair

Almost overnight the Prefab village had become a reality. Where acres of bomb-scarred rubble had previously existed, low lines of rectangular light-grey structures occupied the land. The areas surrounding, (the gardens to be, that is), were covered in a dark sea of dreary looking clinker. This was the council's clumsy attempt to impose some kind of uniformity on the half-buried boulders of concrete, broken prams and stumps of foundation walls left over from the previous terraces. Here and there, clumps of silver birch and sycamores had survived the bulldozers, together with patches of rose-brambles, defiantly alive with crimson blossom.

John's family had been one of the first to move into the completed site. He was part of a new breed, 'the Prefab children'. Many were the cartoons that appeared in the popular press with the first appearance of the Prefabs. Couples were depicted in their gardens, desperately holding the roof on with ropes, at the slightest hint of a storm. Some were shown being blown up into space like a flying carpet, with the occupants gazing dumbstruck from the kitchen and bedroom window.

Of course, it was all nonsense. John's family, like their neighbours, enjoyed the sense of space around the detached dwellings and wouldn't now change them for anything, least of all the drab-looking council flats springing up in increasing numbers. Within six months, the new inhabitants had removed cart loads of clinker and substituted in its place rich loam soil from Kent. Now, some five years on, the Prefab village was a place of young shrubs and hollyhocks, golden privet hedges and beds of wallflowers. Under improvised glass frames, lettuce and tomatoes flourished. In retrospect, the housing experiment was a triumphant success.

John lived in the next-but-one dwelling from Ken and the two very quickly became friends. Soon, he met the others and, although he liked them all individually, he was not one for crowds. He was a peripheral member of the group. It was inconceivable that he might accompany the others for dancing at the Grange, or listen to Ken's idiotic jazz records, as much as he tried to convert him. Johnny Ray was good enough for him. Although he occasionally joined the others for a cricket session, he was not physically very strong, a legacy from his father who had retired early in poor health.

Where he did excel was in the making of aeroplane models and this was his great part-time passion. It was more fun for him to decorate the fuselage of a Messerschmitt 109 than to stroll around East-Lane market with the others on a Sunday. Being an only child he enjoyed the privileges it gave him, the privacy of his own bedroom for one. He had turned it into a wonderland of suspended models, all beautifully detailed. Spitfires with cantilever wings, Stuka dive-bombers with sinister big wheels and the graceful shape of the Sunderland Flying Boat, (he was particularly pleased with this). Surrounded by all these, he didn't really need the company of the others on a regular basis.

He had heard the gossip about the new girl and had scoffed at it. Pat? Pauline? Penny? So what! His father grew tomatoes to sell locally in a modest way and Pat's parents had ordered a couple of pounds. John had the job of delivering them and found himself face to face with the girl that had caused a few dozen tongues to wag, if not a thousand ships to sail.

His first reaction to Pat, was one of relief. After all he had heard about her, he had expected a bewitching siren. She was not even beautiful but, as they exchanged a few words over the price and the quality of the fruit, John thought here is a girl I could enjoy doing simple things with.

'Dad's got some lettuce, they're beauties. He's lifting them on Saturday morning. Why don't you come over and take first pick.'

'OK thanks! I'll tell them,' she replied and departed inside with the tomatoes.

Pat was beginning to remember the faces of the local boys quite well by now but had only exchanged a few words with one of them and that was Geoffrey in the street cricket knockabout. She thought her dad might well want some lettuce this coming weekend and stored away the notion that she would be the carrier as well as the messenger.

She was now acquainted with two of the boys that seemed to be the local gang. They certainly weren't what she thought they would be like, before she moved into the district. Her friends had told her Bermondsey was full of barrow boys and Teddy boys but this was only partly true. She found there a solid core of hard-working youngsters who, after a long week of labour in factories, offices, wharves and breweries, wanted to get as much fun out of the short weekends as they could, before the Monday morning grind started up again. Things seemed to happen much faster here.

In some ways the local girls were much saucier than the boys, who showed interest in a warm and often witty way, unlike the former, who eyed her with suspicion. Sometimes a group of four girls would march down the road arm in arm, throwing haughty looks in her direction. They looked more dangerous than the boys and she felt she would never become part of their world, however long she lived there. She would always be an outsider.

That same evening, John was meeting the others for a special night out. The travelling fair had arrived again on its twice yearly visit to the local park. It was an enormous affair that filled most of the oval. Only one visit was usually possible for the boys. Not because they had exhausted the excitement it offered, far from it. The reason was more down to earth. They saved for the event weeks in advance and when the night came, spent the lot in a glorious binge of dodgem cars, ghost trains, helter-skelter and Big Lizzie rides, as well as the numerous sideshows, so hard to resist. After a night at the fair, they were well and truly broke but it was a night to remember!

The boys met in their usual place, outside the bicycle shop and moved off towards the park As they strolled along, Ken narrated the gist of some recent gossip.

'I heard a funny thing today in school. Last Saturday, one of the Brick Gang got duffed up by the fairground boys. It was over some prize he thought he should have won, or something! Anyway, Sullivan heard it from his brother that the Brick boys are going to pull the place apart tonight.'

'We've picked the right night then,' Geoffrey laughed, 'it sounds like it's going to be a rough-house. I think I'll stay on the ghost-train all evening.'

'Sullivan reckoned they're going in strength,' Ken added and the topic was put aside as they came in sight of the flashing lights delineating the castellated roofs of the high-flying roundabouts.

Deafening music blazed out, above and beyond the immediate vicinity of the fair. TROOLY-TROOLY FAIR-TROOLY-TROOLY-FAIR - HOW I LUV-MY-TROOLY-FAIR! Guy Mitchell's latest hit pounded away in competition with Frankie Laine's' 'MULE TRAIN-MOOL TRAIN-CLIPPETY-CLOPPING-OVER-HILL AND DALE!' Above even this noise, the screams of terrified girls rose in chorus, as the roller-coaster dipped and plunged. It was a battlefield scene, without the slaughter.

Intoxicated by the highly charged atmosphere, the boys jumped onto a grand affair of a roundabout called 'Whiplash'. Sitting inside a hollowed out duck-of-a-carriage, they gripped the brass handrail expectantly. The music changed tempo and they began to circulate slowly. The sense of motion was most experienced by the sight of the carriage in front, a giant goldfish carrying two girls. Clinging closely together, they waved bravely to friends below, as a secondary rhythm of up-and-down bobbing complemented the wider gyrations.

A man leapt skilfully from one party to another, collecting money and hardly pausing as the roundabout picked up speed. All passengers were now flying out at a tangent, high above the heads of onlookers. These soon became nothing but a blur and everyone concentrated hard on survival. Holding on tight did prevent you from being flung, like a missile, into outer space but what if you had cramp or something? These thoughts flashed through John's mind, as they undoubtedly did to the other joyriders. Would you land in a bush, or on the canvas roof of another sideshow?

As different as they were as individuals, the riders shared one thing in common. Sweet/sour, love/hate, danger/safety, it was the attraction of extremes which brought them all together in this moment of madness.

Within the regulations and constraints of society, it was necessary to go out of control once in a while.

The 'Whiplash' slowed in tempo. Golden cockerels, ducks and the other baroque carriages all obeyed the rules of gravity and dropped to a perpendicular plumb as the music also slackened in volume. Shakily, the joy-riders dismounted and fell into the embraces of the fringe of sisters, mothers, brothers and lovers all waiting below.

The fair was very crowded. Strings of boisterous youngsters ran twisting through parties of shuffling elders. A group of four girls crossed their path, waving a stuffed teddy bear in their direction. Ken identified one of them as Hazel, a girl he had dated several times in the past. All the girls wore the same style, suits, cleanly cut in silver/grey gabardine. Long lapels plunged down sharply pressed jacket fronts, the hems of which were finger-tip in length. The boys shuffled aimlessly in their footsteps, not so much following them as drifting along in the general current of the crowd.

Imperceptibly, they were overtaken by a large group of youths, some of whom wore yellow football shirts. As they drew abreast of the 'Haunted House' on their left, a sudden surge to the right carried the main mob around a slide-penny booth. As if by a prearranged signal, two youths leapt onto the counter of the booth and tap-danced their way across its surface, scattering columns of coins in all directions.

'Go to it Sammy Boy, score for Millwall.'

In mock obedience, one of them seized a pink panda bear and booted it high over the heads of the crowd. The stall owner grabbed the other toys stacked at the rear and bundled them out of sight below the counter, yelling for help as she did so.

'We better get out of here, it's the Brick Gang,' shouted Geoffrey, but that was easier said than done. More people had crushed up behind them, anxious not to miss the excitement and it was only by squeezing down a narrow path between the 'Haunted House' and a stationery caravan that they were able to extricate themselves. Hazel and her three friends followed the boys' example, all four picking a passage through the guy-ropes, petrol cans and wooden beams.

Even as the boys left, the cries for help had brought a tough-looking

ensemble of men, armed with tent spars and mallets. It was clear by their quick reaction, that they had been expecting trouble and had worked out a counter-offensive. All hell broke loose as the two sides piled into each other. The sounds of ripping canvas, yells and barking dogs rose above the scene. After ten minutes the sharp sound of a whistle cut the air. It was the fall-back signal of the Brick Gang and within seconds they had all melted into the crowds and the fight was over, as suddenly as it had begun.

John and his friends reached the far side of the fair in time to see an orderly retreat. In the dusk light, a long column of youths, thirty strong at least, unhurriedly made their way towards the park gates. The oval was otherwise silent and devoid of people. Even as they watched, the night closed in, reducing all to an indigo blanket.

The following day, the word had passed through the grapevine. Geoffrey acting as harbinger. Highly excited, he shared the news. 'Guess what? An amazing thing happened afterwards. When the gang left the park, they caught a tram to the Old Kent Road and guess what? The police drew a patrol car across the tracks, another car came up behind and the gang was trapped. The police bundled them off the tram and straight into Tower Bridge Street Police Station opposite and that's only half of it! They made them an offer! Either sign on for three years in the Army or spend two years in a Borstal Institution.'

'That's fantastic,' John said, 'what a choice!'

'Yeah, but what would you choose in their shoes?'

'That's easy,' Ken joined in. 'They're bound to take the Army. If they survive the square-bashing, they'll end up being nasty little corporals, bossing everyone around.'

'It will be our rotten luck if they get the same posting as us,' said John.

'I think I'll put down for the Far East.'

'The farther the better,' yelled the others in unison.

'One thing's for sure, they won't get into the Air Force. There's not enough Brylcreem in the whole RAF to keep that lot going.'

Geoffrey

It was August bank holiday again and London was beginning to look decidedly empty. Many families had already left for their annual seaside holiday but Geoffrey's family was not one of these. They never went away. Indeed, the furthest his mother had managed was Bromley High Street and this only because it was where the No. 1 bus ended its route.

Sometimes in past years, Geoffrey and his elder brother Stacey, had been loaned to Uncle Bill and Aunt Ethel, to strengthen their hop-picking team. They always went to the same place, East Peckham, in Kent. At least this was a change of scene, if not a holiday. Toiling day after day for a week, filling the long bins with hops from the freshly cut vines required a lot of stamina and also tolerance of the company you were confined with.

Geoffrey like his relatives with their free and easy conversation, they usually turned the whole affair into a party but, most of all, he relished the sweet air of the Kentish countryside. It reminded him of the country schools he had visited in the cricket season. Even his worst enemy had to admit Geoffrey was a talented player, an all-rounder with the ability to bat hard, as well as send the ball down at a cracking pace. He had played in St. Joseph's school team for the last two consecutive seasons and they were lucky to have him. It could be said, the term all-rounder, described his whole personality very adequately, prepared as he so often was, to jump in and try things out, when others held back.

Both brothers had been invited again to join the hop-picking expedition but nobody expected Stacey to accept, he had only been nine months out of the army and, in any case, he was too involved with his work on the river.

Geoffrey eagerly agreed however, although he did not particularly fancy the idea of sleeping by himself in the tent he always used in preference to the stuffy wooden huts that served as homes to the pickers.

There was also another reason he would rather be under canvas. His aunt and uncle were the salt of the earth and he would not hear a word said against them but his affection could not overcome the chorus of snoring that blasted through their bedroom door, shattering the peaceful night air. This constant barrage could only be tolerated by the deaf. Sucking and wheezing sounds rattled the thin wooden partitions until the two brothers in despair had taken to sitting outside. Later, exhausted, they retired to oblivious slumber.

Geoffrey had found the use of a tent the ideal solution but, hitherto, there had always been the company of Stacey or his cousin Jake. One had outgrown the whole event and the other had just been called up to serve in the RAF.

It was with these thoughts in mind that he approached his close friends Ken and Sandy to join him for the Kentish trip.

'It's always sunny there! You can get brown very quickly,' he said, in a cunning appeal to Ken's vanity.

'What about the food?' Sandy asked.

'You can have rabbit stew, or cornish pasties, there's tons of grub, cider and beer as well, all free!' With Geoffrey's persuasive replies, Ken and Sandy were soon won over and they all got down to sorting out their travel arrangements.

It would certainly be different. Neither Ken nor Sandy's parents had ever been part of the hop-picking crowd, it was all a bit too 'Gipsy'. Both fathers had worked as under-managers in a car showroom and furniture store respectively. A week in Bournemouth was more to their taste.

The time for the trip soon came and all three found themselves enjoying the leisurely pace of the train as it chugged out of London Bridge Station and made its way through the suburbs of South London and into open country. The sharp cream and brown houses of stockbrokers' Tudor, gave way to farms and artisan cottages as they passed from Orpington to Sevenoaks and beyond. At last they reached Paddock Wood from where they continued by bus.

Ken and Sandy had already agreed they would only stay the weekend, in spite of Geoffrey's pleas to see the week out. They hadn't a clue what to expect. 'Something between a marsh and a jungle,' Ken joked privately. When they stopped off the bus at East Peckham, they were both amazed at the neatness of it all. Fields with lines of tall poles, all dead straight, traversed the surrounding areas, sometimes marching up a slight incline all festooned with the luxurious loops and arabesques of the vines. A malty sweet scent pervaded the air. Further afield whitewashed houses peeped out from behind apple orchards and the dark yew trees of a churchyard.

Their dwelling to be was one of a group of huts slotted into a waste patch between the fields, well sheltered from the winds by a belt of low trees. Neither Ken nor Sandy had been to the country since evacuation ten years before in the War and time had distorted their perception. They stared at the pattern of orchards and vineyards and marvelled at the logic of it all. It hadn't occurred to them, they were only thirty five miles from London.

On the threshold of the hut, Aunt Ethel greeted them warmly, waving a pot of tea with one arm and hugging the boys with the other. The hut was roomier inside than it looked from without. Such was the cunning layout, much had been packed within its limits. An array of enamel mugs and colourful china plates lined the shelves over the cooking area. The feeling was more like that on board a ship, than in a bungalow. Bottles of brown ale and stout stood ready on the scrubbed pine table and something else, which turned out to be Eno's Fruit Salts, rather than the lemonade Ken mistook it for. The crab sandwiches were delicious and disappeared at the speed of light. Apple tart followed, richly covered in thick custard. It was certainly a feast!

Uncle Bill produced a portable wind-up gramophone and, getting into the party spirit, proceeded to play his favourite records. These were all in the manner of witty-ditties. 'The Laughing Policeman', they had all heard before but another number was new to them. In it, a sad Lancashire voice narrated the tale of Sam and his 'Brown Boots'. So much did they like it, Uncle Bill played it again. *Brown Boots, I ask yer! Brown Boots, when all the rest were wearing black!'* The victim, it seemed, had committed the unpardonable sin of attending his relative's funeral in the wrong coloured shoes. The record continued *'We didn't know, he didn't say, he gave his other shoes away!'* (To someone who had no shoes at all, it transpired) but his sacrifice was discovered all too late, the poor fellow just couldn't win. Uncle Bill burst into pretend tears and they all fell about laughing.

The evening was passing quickly and Geoffrey announced the time had come to put up the tent, before the light faded. Since he was the only one with any experience of such things, he put himself in the role of group leader. Firstly, he had to select the right spot to pitch tent and, after a show of patting the grass to feel any bumps, opted for a spot which looked exactly the same as the surrounding areas, contoured as they were with ridges and furrows.

The tent went up without difficulty, although it seemed a bit small. This was not surprising as it was only designed for two. However, it looked strong enough and able to defy the worst weather they might expect but they were lucky. Day after day, the sun beat down with great generosity, causing Aunt Ethel to remark with satisfaction on the quick drying time needed for the host of socks and shirts suspended from the improvised line.

As well as a groundsheet, they each had a sleeping bag and felt confident they could withstand anything the wilds of Kent might send their way. As dusk turned to night, they chatted on about this and that, until Ken suddenly jerked upright.

'It's a bug!' he yelled. 'It's gone into my sleeping bag.' The others screamed in mock terror and an immediate inspection was launched to find the threat to their sleep, if not their lives.

'What did it look like?' asked Geoffrey.

'A kind of rusty blood-red,' Ken replied, as Sandy edged as far away as he could from the others. He had never been good with insects.

All agreed, the problem was to extricate the creature without squashing it, the consequences of which would be a technicolour juicy stain.

'I've got it, in my handkerchief, I'm throwing it outside.' Ken could not execute the creature even if he tried. There literally was no space to do so without causing more problems.

'Show it!' yelled Geoffrey and, as it came from out of a fold in Ken's hand, he triumphantly declared, 'It's an earywig! It's got a stinger on its bottom, watch it twist up,' and proved it with a touch of a twig. Any further inspection was thwarted by Ken's determined run for the flap-door and his flick of the insect into the grass beyond.

As all three settled down again to lie staring at the ridgepole above their heads, Geoffrey put the question: 'Do you know why they call them earywigs?'

'No,' the other two replied in unison.

'Why should we?' added Sandy defensively.

'Well, you see they go for your ear, crawl right in, that's why they call them earywigs.' This revelation was greeted in silence for some moments while the implications sank in.

'Look, you must be wrong, 'cos they couldn't get past the eardrum,' Sandy emphasised his challenge with a savage jab at a dark patch on the canvas above him. Two large moths flapped away in confusion.

'Yes and another thing, they would probably get lost, take the wrong passage or something. It must be like Piccadilly tube station in there.' Geoffrey had elaborated, rather than withdrawn his argument.

Ken had lain silent so far but he had heard enough and, being a grammar school boy, had worked out an answer.

'Of course they know where to go all right, they are like guided missiles, attracted by the heat of the brain. First thing tomorrow I'm asking Aunt Ethel for some cotton wool, it's the only way to stop them. Once they're in you're finished.'

With that, all three fell into a deep sleep, that even the dawn chorus of squawking geese could not disturb.

Nocturnal rustlings of mice and hedgehogs gave way to the sweet fresh smells of the new day. The sun resplendent, climbed the cerulean blue sky and the boys joined the elders for breakfast. The first night had been, what you might call, an educational experience.

Later, all three presented themselves to Aunt Ethel. She managed to keep a straight face and, although she laughed about it for years afterwards, she inwardly sympathised with their predicament. After all, why were they called earywigs?

Ken

Ken kept very still. Beneath the laurel shrub where he lay with Sheila, they were well hidden but the tramp of a dozen feet or so was too close for comfort.

It had been Sheila's idea, to crawl through the broken fence into the shrubbery at the oval end of the park. Wednesday was always a dull night at St. Luke's Youth Club. Most of Ken's friends were at New Cross Speedway, a sport which left him cold, so, after a few jives to Buddy Holly records, Sheila's sly invitation, murmured out of earshot of the others, seemed full of promise.

Not that he particularly fancied Sheila, he told himself, although she was well set up. From a trim waist, long thighs curved down to finely carved ankles. Bronze buckled shoes of Italian gold leather completed the effect. He had noticed her shoulders earlier, they didn't slope weakly away like so many of her generation but maintained a taught square line, supported by a flat back and a more than adequate front.

Ken liked her style. She was one of the Lyceum regulars and took great pains to show others that the club was only a fill-in until Saturday night came, when the magic of Oscar Rabin's band and the moonbeam rays reflecting from the faceted sphere high above the dancers, transported all beneath to a neverworld of fantasy and romance.

After Pat, she was the best girl around. An hour earlier, as they looped and spun in figure eight turns, he noticed how her wide-necked blouse would just manage to stay on her shoulders, pulling the taffeta in diagonal creases across her breasts.

He could hardly, therefore, resist her tempting invite, which had stepped up the pace in what had been, up till then, a general friendship.

15

Their leaving together would certainly have been noticed by the club's small fry and made the subject of speculative gossip.

Dancing, table-tennis, chat over tea and cakes, this was the eternal pattern of social life at the club and Ken was beginning to tire of it.

His National Service started in three months and there seemed nothing else to do until that time came. Fights were rare at the club and those looking for trouble seldom came by. It was also good for the chance it gave to meet the opposite sex in relaxed surroundings, although he wished there was more choice.

In this circle, Sheila stood out from the crowd. It wasn't her way to slavishly follow trends like the Teddy-girl fashion. She would, instead, adapt it to bring out the best in her lithe form.

Black velvet collar and pearl choker necklace were obligatory but her drape jacket was cut at a sensible finger-tip length and her make-up was restrained without that opaque pancake look all too common.

Sheila really was OK. There was only one thing wrong: Ken was in love with Pat. His closest friends, Sandy, Geoff and John were also in love with Pat, sharing that state with at least twenty other boys in the neighbourhood.

Pat was something else! She had come into the district from the outer suburbs and didn't speak like a Londoner. She was the only teenager for miles around to so casually ignore the latest fashion, preferring instead to dress in daintily patterned full skirts.

Whereas most of the local girls clattered about, arm in arm, in groups, Pat was a loner. She knew nobody in the area, this made her appear more innocent and, at once, more desirable.

Everything about her was so different. Her parents were hardly ever seen, unlike the locals, busily tending their postage stamp gardens and gossiping over the front gate. She was their only child. Desperate and quite ingenuous attempts to make her acquaintance were made by every male from fifteen to twenty five who lived in the tight network of nearby streets.

She was sixteen and had entered their lives as if from another planet. To meet her in a normal way proved quite difficult but one day a breakthrough came about. Adjacent to her terraced cottage, a stretch of vacant wall provided the boys with a chalked-up wicket and a long stretch of road to practise cricket.

It was Geoffrey who hit the ball that travelled some thirty yards and ended its flight at her front door. Dismay turned to expectation, as a minute passed before the door pushed cautiously open. A cloud of golden hair and eyes with just a hint of amusement in them stood at the threshold. Their first encounter had begun.

In an unusual move for a batsman, Geoffrey had already run some paces to retrieve the ball.

'Sorry, I hope I didn't wake you up,' he offered as an opening shot. She smiled back but did not answer and gently closed the door. Nothing further was seen of her for a week or two.

Ken was brought abruptly out of his musing and into the dangerous present as the sound of a stick savagely swished through the bough which extended over their heads to overhang the tarmac path that coursed its way around the oval. Sheila leaned into him as they both flattened as best they could in the undergrowth beneath the shrub.

Nervously, they lay in the damp, hardly daring to breathe but they were not seen and the shuffling feet diminished into the other sounds of the night; the hooting of the tugs from Surrey Docks and the whistle of the biscuit factory summoning the late shift to work.

Now the danger was past he could think clearly. He was sure the passing group were members of the Brick Gang, the most dreaded lot imaginable. They dominated the areas between the Old Kent Road and the Bricklayers Arms pub, (thus their name). Their influence had now spread into London Bridge in the north and Peckham Rye Lane in the south. With the support of satellite gangs, they were said to be at least three hundred strong. It was best to keep well out of their way, avoiding known stamping grounds such as the dance halls by the Peckham canal and the Saturday night Elephant and Castle crowd, lingering late after the cinemas closed.

'What would you have done if they had caught us?' Sheila asked suddenly. Ken had asked himself the same question five times earlier and had not come up with any answers. He had to convince Sheila he could manage things and, surprised by his own glibness, answered, 'I know Pascoe, he works in my dad's garage. I would have told them Pascoe's my mate.'

This was in essence true. There was a time, long before Pascoe got involved with the Brick Gang, when they were quite friendly. Pascoe then changed. He seemed to become a different person and began mixing with the Elephant and Castle mob. Ken saw little of him now, although they still had a good laugh whenever they did happen to meet.

Pascoe's standing was very high. He was famous in the south east for his boxing skills, taking the Junior Championship for two consecutive years. Probably Ken's plan in seeking the protection of his name would have been enough to turn aside the potential aggression of any random encounter. The gang tended to pick on victims who were less vocal and not possessing such powerful allies. They would just give them a beating for the fun of it, preferably with an audience of satellite girls to impress.

'Why didn't you join them when Pascoe did?'

'I don't like tramping around in big crowds,' and boastingly added, 'I prefer to go to up town solo and have a good night in a jazz club. All they know about is causing bother.'

This answer wasn't strictly true. If he could, he would go with a dancing partner and, in this respect, he had been lucky to have the company of a young Jewish hairdresser. Unfortunately she had now become engaged to someone in her trade and that had ended nine months of beautiful dancing, where they had coordinated their jiving to a fine art.

It had left Ken in something of a vacuum. Looking at Sheila, he wondered if she would fit into the more bohemian atmosphere of the basement jazz clubs of Soho. She had the presence and, with a bit of polishing up, she might well replace his loss. Taking her jiving would not mean she was his 'girl'.

The patrons of the jazz club had evolved a very flexible understanding on this. It all combined to make a convivial atmosphere in which many combinations of partners, lovers and just good friends all managed to have a good time. Jazz on a Saturday night was always the highlight of the week. Also, being in love with Pat would not preclude taking Sheila dancing, as they were on such different levels and poles apart. The world of Soho and the world of Surrey Docks, as different as Iceland and Greece.

Almost before he realised, he found himself inviting her. 'Will you come dancing on Saturday?' Humphrey Littleton's band are playing.'

This name meant nothing to Sheila but she knew this was an offer of a different sort of night out and she readily accepted with a quick, 'What shall I wear?'.

Ken's hand inched up her blouse and stopped short of her left breast.

'Why don't you wear your black drainpipes with a stripey top,' he replied and edged his hand an inch higher. Sheila then pushed tight against him, making it clear that all conversation was suspended for some while.

They had now entered a phase with very clear ground rules. It was OK to go all the way if you were engaged or if a more permanent understanding existed but to make love in a casual sense was asking for it. To Ken and his crowd it meant living a kind of lie, unfair on the girl and equally difficult for the boy, who would have to fend off pressure to get married and settle down properly. In the interim would be the, *where do we live?* questions followed by the *steady job prospects* or lack of, more likely.

Things needn't be so complicated. You take a girl out. You enjoy yourselves and go as far as you can, without the ultimate move. Not that the girls didn't expect the boys to try. There was spicy glamour in being described as a 'fast one'. It projected an image of worldly experience and confidence which most girls preferred to the mumbling fumblings of a novice. The trick was - and Ken believed this wholeheartedly - to appear fast without actually being so. To cool it off at the point where the girl was begging him to stop with her tongue but sending opposite signals with her lips.

Sheila was elated. For two months she had schemed to make a date with Ken and now it had happened. She remembered the first time they met. It was in the canteen of St. Luke's. Somebody was giving a very funny impression of Marlon Brando as Mark Anthony, to the delight of the others. A youth with honey-blonde hair and a very striking profile was making dramatic gestures whilst wearing a raincoat in reverse. The exposed red lining draped across his chest to form a crude toga. In a strangled nasal accent, the lines rang out, 'I come to bury Caesar not to praise him. The bad men do lives on after them, the good is oft interred with their bones,' at that point somebody threw a jam doughnut across the room and the performance ended in more chaos than it had begun.

From that time on, Sheila saw in Ken an unusually exciting personality. Although he was certainly a handsome boy, it didn't always follow that the good-looking ones were very bright, as her last boyfriend had proved. He was tall in stature, athletic in build and very serious in his intentions towards her.

How her friends had envied their romance. After three months it had reached the point where they were considering an engagement but, as the weeks went by, she discovered he could talk about nothing else but the family business. This was the breeding and racing of greyhounds, an unusual cottage industry, even for Bermondsey. As the racetrack was at New Cross, less than half a mile away, hardly a moment went by when the conversation was not about the 'dogs'. What was worse, he insisted on her accompanying him two nights a week to watch their hounds perform. She found herself dreading the whole spectacle - the floodlit crowds in grey raincoats, the starting gate clanging open and the mechanical hare gradually being overtaken by the streaking mass. A senseless ritual, repeated night after night, week after week.

She could see the future with him very clearly. She would be marrying a racetrack as much as a man. Sheila ended the affair swiftly and without remorse. There was no time for false sentiment in her world, it either worked or it didn't.

Ken couldn't have been more different. For one thing, he was more educated than most of the boys she knew. He had been to grammar school and had a wider outlook on life. She sensed he was the type who got bored very quickly with one person.

She would have to devise ways to make herself more interesting and different from the others. At least her Lyceum nights had given her a greater degree of sophistication in dealings with the opposite sex. She had become quite skilled at reading the signals and anticipating how a situation might develop. Tonight was a big breakthrough and, with a bit of cunning and gentle persuasion, she might yet make it with Ken.

There was a puritan streak running through Ken and Sheila's generation. When the right time came, they would know and do the right thing. It would be a magnificent occasion and, like their parents' marriages, it would last forever.

Sheila suddenly wriggled free of her pointed bra. She wasn't sure whether he had unhooked the fasteners or she had. Her breasts were now his to fondle for as long as he could stand it and that would be quite a time. She lay back with her eyes closed and neither of them spoke again until much later.

Down by the Riverside

As John stared across the river he became increasingly aware that both feet were slowly sinking in the mud. Gingerly extracting himself, he moved to a patch of shingle close by where he could still focus on the two objects of his attention. The first was on the opposite bank of the Thames at Wapping, where the River Police maintained a busy fleet of launches and the second was the figures of three boys clambering over a clump of barges moored just yards from where he stood. The first three of these lay solidly on the mud bank but the fourth was partly afloat with the incoming tide and soon the waters would lift all the craft, to clang and boom against each other with the ebb and flow of the current.

John had always been aware of the dangers of the river and had refused to join Ken, Sandy and Geoffrey in exploring the barges. Not only was it difficult to climb up the mooring ropes to reach the decks, there was also the question of being caught and accused of stealing. Many of the gangs to whom the shore was a playground did help themselves to handfuls of peanuts or, better still sugar barley, if some craft had carelessly been left uncovered but that wasn't his friends' interest at all. They were simply testing their climbing skills and exploring generally. In any case, all the hatches were battened firmly down, so there was no question of being tempted even.

By now Geoffrey had reached the furthermost barge, floating free of the bank and bobbing up and down gently as the others made tentative passage across the decks to join him.

John's remaining on the bank was not entirely through his nervous disposition. A sharp lookout was necessary as the lightermen might return at any moment. Also, the Police launches on the far bank were adept at cruising silently over to catch those with an adventurous nature unawares. To the crew, it was simply a question of discouraging the persistent offenders in what, after all, was a dangerous pastime.

Geoffrey was shouting something to him but it was carried on the wind and only partly heard.

'Spread out like a big white dog?' was all John could make sense of, then he saw the launch. It had not crossed the river but had crept up from the west, partly hidden by the next tier of barges. Black and full of purpose it edged closer to where Geoffrey, unaware, intently studied a light patch floating just a short distance away. The Police launch saw it also and giving up all attempt at surprise revved up speed to pull alongside the unidentified object. There was no need for John to shout a warning, all three had jumped down the

mooring ropes and now stood beside him, surveying the drama offshore.

Then events took a fast turn. Within minutes they were joined on the beach by three constables dressed in oilskin high boots and carrying a stretcher. The launch steered as close as possible to the shore and the newly arrived officers waded out to meet it. From the higher vantage point they watched as the uniformed group prodded the water and dragged on board what appeared to be a misshapen white blanket.

'Probably a sheep that's fallen in further down river,' Ken speculated. To them floating carcasses were nothing new. At various times they had seen dogs, pigs and even cows floating in with the tide but they weren't quite prepared for what they saw next.

Some sort of discussion went on around the launch and the object, heavy and shapeless was conveyed over the side to the waiting stretcher party. Out of the water and up the bank they squelched and as they passed the boys it happened. From the stretcher a long sinewy arm fell, fingers outstretched and dangling in the mud.

The constables rested their load and moving the sheet back attempted to replace the arm. Momentarily, they caught sight of a crazed face, grinning from ear to ear. Mercifully, the eyes were closed and the sheet was hastily replaced to cover the wreck of a body. As the cortege resumed its passage, the nauseating stench of rotting flesh filled the air. John felt himself about to faint and grabbed the nearest shoulder. A shout brought him to his senses and he recovered his composure. Retracing the deep imprints of the policemen up the beach, the boys reached the quay in time to see them depart in a high-windowed van.

Leaving the river, a brighter mood set in.

"We should all go to Brighton for a day,' Geoffrey ventured. 'It would make a change from Bermondsey. They've got that big 'Pop-Eye' on the promenade, the one that laughs.'

'What about Olive Oil, is she there too?' Sandy asked. 'No Olive Oil, no Brighton!'

Having come to an agreement of sorts, they made their way home. The macabre event of a few moments ago was already slipping into history.

Doorstep Romeo

John studied the freshly cut row of lettuces on the kitchen table and chose the fattest one he could find. Today he had a mission to fulfil. His father's home-grown vegetables were finding plenty of nearby customers and on Saturdays he found himself cast in the role of delivery boy.

Amongst these grateful recipients were Pat's parents, both fond of a salad at weekends and living just a stone's throw away from his own Prefab. Throughout the week he had eagerly anticipated this moment and had timed it to perfection. He knew that all in her house were regular Millwall supporters and the only place they were likely to be on a Saturday afternoon, was at that holy of holies, the Den.

This was his third delivery to date and he was beginning to know their routines. He knew that if he waited till after lunch he would be sure to find Pat alone. His legitimate errands had put him well ahead of Ken and Sandy in the race for Pat's attention and he relished the thought. In these fleeting interludes he had struck up an easy line of conversation and with time he hoped it would grow into something much more. Of course, the others were after her too and there was always the chance he would be outmanoeuvred. In this respect, Ken was the biggest threat.

In conversation with his friends John would play down any suggestion of contact, feigning disinterest but his tete-a-tetes had not gone unnoticed.

'They must be vegetarians in her house, the stuff you've sold them this month,' Sandy teased but John refused to be drawn.

'Perhaps they keep rabbits out the back.' Geoffrey's eyes glazed over at the thought. 'Rabbit stew is my favourite!'

'Why don't you ask her yourself, she doesn't say much to me.' John's irritable reply ended their search for any scrap of information they might glean about the new face in the street and the topic was dropped.

John had already rehearsed his meeting with Pat. By chance, a hilarious incident had occurred in his company office which had supplied him with an entertaining line of conversation.

He had noticed previously how easy she was to impress and mentally polished his story to make it all the funnier. Scanning the road from end to end and seeing no sign of the others he strode up to Pat's door and knocked boldly. Seconds later, in a swirling creamy coloured dress, Pat stood smiling within the threshold.

'Oooh, that's nice! Wait a minute, I'll just fetch the money.' This last remark was quite unnecessary as she knew John hadn't the slightest intention of going anywhere.

John straightened his tie and awaited his cue. Before regaining the front door, Pat paused by the mirror in the hall and gently pushed her hair this way and that. She enjoyed John's transparently obvious attempts to 'chat her up' but she wished she could meet his other friends also. From her upstairs window she had witnessed dangerously bravado displays of cycling, speedway style. One foot dragging in the dust, the boys leaned their bikes over in defiance of all the laws of gravity, chasing around the crudely chalked lines. The fact they had created their track on the road just twenty yards below, was a sure sign they were trying to impress her but she had yet to find the means to make their acquaintance without seeming too forward. The two she had yet to meet looked the most interesting of the gang.

Sensing the right moment, John launched into his comic tale. It transpired that several of his workmates had concocted an April Fools joke on another member of the firm, a rather quiet withdrawn character called Fred who spoke very little and declined to take part in any of the social events which helped cement the office fraternity together as a community, if not as friends.

Pat's eyes flashed appreciatively and John continued.

'It all started with Ernie. He's the joker, always playing pranks on us. Well.... this time he went too far! This bloke Fred, he works in the next office to me,' and with an extra flourish of technical expertise, continued, 'He's very good at languages. He speaks German and Danish, so they put him in charge of all exports to the Baltic.' It seemed that Ernie, 'a life and soul of the party' type, was particularly annoyed by Fred's reticence to join the office coach trip to Brighton. When invited Fred had made the excuse that he needed all his spare cash for his holiday to Hamburg.

As so often happens to a work-force confined together on humdrum routines, what started as a light-hearted niggle, grew into open hostility at Fred's stubborn independence.

'I wouldn't mind,' Ernie moaned to the others, 'we put a lot of effort into the Brighton do and the firm's paying for it anyway! What's so special about Hamburg I'd like to know?'

'It's near Russia ain't it? Perhaps he's got a Fraulein there,' said another. In great detail, John went on to narrate the whole saga, as Pat's curiosity grew by the minute. Amongst Ernie's circle, the 'Russian' remark sparked off an idea and soon a plot began to form which would shake Fred's indifference once and for all.

There was no doubt a degree of envy existed amongst some in the office at Fred's ability to learn other languages but it had never manifested itself in such an open, or, it must be said, imaginative way before. Someone alluded to Fred's habit of sitting by himself reading obscure magazines, while the others were busy discussing the previous night's telly.

'It's unnatural, honest! He's the only person I know who doesn't watch 'What's My Line'!' Ernie exclaimed indignantly.

An unstopable head of steam was building up, with recriminations such as *Him and his bills of lading. He thinks he's above us!' 'Yeah! Why can't he acknowledge his work mates? He's nothing special. A few fancy languages, that's all!'*

Then Ernie came up with his brainwave. 'I know, let's send a letter to his wife, pretending it's from the Russian Embassy.' This idea was greeted with glee. 'Oh, that's a good one Ern. Let's get a stamp off the Polish bills and stick it on the envelope.'

'Ha! Ha! Yeah, she won't know the difference!'

Spurred on by Pat's rapt attention, John was quite carried away by his narration.

'So they cooked up this letter to look like a thank you note from Russia about exports of guns to some place in the East, all written in funny English. It alleged 'Agent Fred' was to receive money from a contact in Hamburg.'

'Oooh, that was a clever thing to say but wouldn't it get him into trouble?' Pat asked, both shocked and intrigued by it all. 'Supposing someone else had seen it? ....He might have been arrested.'

'It's funny you should say that!' That's exactly what did happen.' John grinned at the audacity of what he was about to reveal.

'Our typist, she lives in the same street as Fred, so I know more than the others what happened. I can tell you, when his wife got the letter, it caused a right to-do. Ernie's forgery was so convincing she didn't know whether to believe it or not.'

'What, her own husband?' Pat found it difficult to accept such disloyalty.'

'Oh, I dunno, the typist says they never go out together but even so, she shouldn't have shown it to her brother, him being a constable at Paradise Street Police Station.'

'I can't believe it, what happened next?'

'Well, it seems she begged him not to but he took the letter straight away to his Sergeant, who forwarded it to Special Branch and they sent it by patrol car the very same day to MI5 headquarters.'

'Who are they?' Pat asked in all innocence.

'Well I shouldn't really tell you,' adding in a conspiratorial whisper. 'As it happens my uncle does the electricity there, it's a hush hush place, near Big Ben. So don't tell anyone what I've said.'

Pat hadn't a clue what he meant by all of this but with the most sophisticated tone she could muster, replied, 'Oh Yes! I've heard of those people.'

An anxious glance up and down the street informed John that he had Pat to himself for at least the next ten minutes and he continued his story undisturbed.

'That very night a Black Maria pulled up outside Fred's door.'

'What's that?' Pat interrupted.

'It's a Police van they carry dangerous criminals in.' John positively oozed metropolitan worldliness as he drawled his answer through cupped hands. This served the duel purpose of emphasising the grave nature of his message and also prevented a nearby sycamore tree being privy to their shared secret.

'They took Fred away but two detectives stayed on and searched the house from top to bottom. They carried away bundles of paper and an old radio set. It was from his army days in the signals but they took it anyway. The typist saw it all from her bedroom window.'

'Oh, I really feel sorry for him. Surely they found out it was only a joke?'

'Oh yes! They knew he wasn't a spy after the Hamburg Police checked out his photograph and details. The Russian writing wasn't Russian at all. The Germans soon found that out but they found out something else too!'

John paused momentarily as if to gain strength before completing the finale of his tale.

'Go on, what was it they found out?' Pat could hardly contain herself. 'Didn't they let him go?'

'It's just like a film I saw. In Hamburg they ran his photograph through their records and, guess what, they found details of Fred's marriage to a German lady just after the war. I expect he was stationed there. All this time he's had two wives and we thought he was the quiet one. The Police apologised for the fuss over the spy scare and were just about to release him when Hamburg phoned up with their discovery. He was charged straight away with bigamy and then released on bail.'

'Oh God! What a dark horse. I know the film you mean, I saw it too, where he had a wife in two different Ports.' Pat made a note to look it up in her Cinema Album. 'But fancy that happening in real life, to someone you know. You just can't tell about some people.'

'Talking about films, I'm going to the Trocette to see the new Tarzan film, would you like to come?'

Before Pat had time to reply a most unwelcome sight appeared on the horizon. Ken and Geoffrey had turned the corner and were walking rapidly towards them. At all costs he could not allow them to meet Pat and highjack his favoured advantage. As Pat assessed the idea of a date with John she hesitated before answering, unaware of his approaching friends. Within three minutes Ken and Geoffrey would be at their side.

Forced into dramatic action, John stared pointedly at the biscuit factory clock. 'That's done it! I'm in real trouble. I've got to take some tomatoes to the 'Blue Anchor' by three o'clock and it's ten past now.' This was partially true. His father's favourite watering hole were good customers but there were no time limits. Raising his arm in a motion somewhere between a push and a wave, he left Pat with open mouth on the threshold. 'Let me know about seeing the Tarzan film, won't you? I hope you can!'

Even as the last sentence left his lips, he was already on his way. With fifty yards to go, he might just about head them off.

Pat half turned in the hallway, her shouted reply a wasted effort, as John was already out of earshot. This did not concern her too much, in fact it excused her declining his invite.

Tarzan films were not exactly her cup of tea but even if the picture had featured her favourite stars, the answer would still be a polite 'No'!

It wasn't just that John talked too much. He was such a boy still. Just one date together and he would be telling everyone *'she was his girlfriend'*.

Pat yearned for a mature man, someone with a decent job who could impress her without even trying. She was in no rush. At seventeen, time stretched before her like an expanding universe.

She had all the time in the world, as they say.

Sandy

Sandy was the first of the friends to receive his calling-up papers. He had no strong feelings about losing two years of his life in what would be tedious routines most of the time. Being of a quieter nature he had decided to make his spell in the Forces as close to normal life as possible. With this in mind he hoped to join the Pay Corps, a role his present post as Junior Clerk in the biscuit factory had well prepared him for.

Three months before he left for his square bashing camp, a dance was being held at the Grange - a Guy Fawkes event for charity. The Grange was to put on a programme of varied entertainment, with nights of boxing alternating with comedy and the occasional dance to punctuate special weekends.

It attracted a more mature crowd of revellers and Sandy liked this. He felt comfortable in the presence of older people and enjoyed dancing with those his senior in years. He danced well and this was in turn appreciated by his partners. It would act as an appropriate send-off before his final week at home and, like the others, he was really looking forward to it.

The friends had not heard of the band before. Leonardo's Samba Sextette clearly sounded like a Latin American group and would attract a good crowd. Sandy, in common with the other boys, knew the rudimentary steps of most of the Latin dances. He prided himself on being the most skilled of their number. Geoffrey could just about manage. Ken was a bit too flamboyant, a legacy from his jazz dancing but he had really done his homework well and the Cha-cha-cha, Rumba and Samba were all smoothly within his grasp. This made him a highly desirable partner for the opposite sex and his skills were soon noticed in any ballroom, particularly amongst the older women.

They all met on the night at their usual rendezvous, the bicycle shop, equidistant between the homes of all three and started out early, eager to hear the new band. The throng in the foyer looked very promising. Young married couples dressed more soberly, a good assortment of the older generations and a sprinkling of Army and RAF uniforms on leave. Perez Prado's Mambo No.5 throbbed through the ornate glass inner doors and, as the revellers moved in and out, they could see a lively scene with energetic but confused Mambo steps being practised together with a simplified form of jive. It was all going very well.

On the next set of three Samba dances, Geoffrey moved off first. He had spotted a girl he knew who worked in Woolworths and one he often spoke to. Geoffrey was a clumsy dancer but he was enthusiastic Sandy thought and the girl was clearly enjoying it. It would take a kill joy not to. The band were playing their hearts out and it was infectious. This wasn't always the case. Sandy remembered a dance six months before when a tired group of musicians murdered number after number and refused to play requests. It hadn't even occurred to the audience that they may not even be familiar with the numbers asked for. Couples shuffled round in a dull haze and the band was never booked again.

Sandy had spotted his chance, or rather answered the inviting look of a woman of about twenty-five who stood alone, apparently with no company. Accepting his invitation, both stepped forward just in time for the last Samba of the set. Hardly had they walked off the floor when the languorous strains of the Rumba brought the dancers quickly back on the floor. Sandy returned with his partner.

The slower rhythm gave him the opportunity to study her more closely. Her eyes were heavily lidded and widely spaced. Her hair, which was set in short upturned curls looked like a froth of black bubbles. Sandy speculated that she had Spanish blood somewhere back in her family line.

She was certainly an eye-catcher and together they looked a very good pair on the floor. The lilt of the Rumba caused her hips to rise and fall in the most desirable way and she made the most of it. Greedy eyes followed their movements from the casually placed tables at the sides, where those that couldn't dance but liked the atmosphere, would sit smoking and drinking lemonade shandies.

'What's your name?' she asked and, without waiting, 'I'm Clare. Her friendly overture led Sandy into offering her a drink in the interval and the two made their way to the area under the balcony which served as a bar.

'Thanks, I'll have a sweet sherry,' she said and moved towards the comfortable seats in deep shadow at the back of the hall.

'Do you live local!' Clare asked.

'Not far, by the Blue Anchor,' Sandy answered. 'How about you?'

'I'm in a flat by the park gates,' she murmured. 'It's very cosy.'

Sandy couldn't quite get the measure of her. Most women of her age were married with at least one youngster and yet, although her face already showed the lines of experience, she didn't look like a mother. Her dress was a pencil-tight sheath in the latest Chinese Lotus style. Sandy knew this because he had seen Elizabeth Taylor wearing one in a recent film. He noticed also, as she lifted her glass, there were no rings on her left hand. Clare caught his glance, 'I left my husband last year. He was a right villain. I'm by myself now.'

Sandy was unprepared for anything like this. Of all the boys, his was the most sheltered background. He had led a very regular, rather routine existence and didn't often encounter the spicy side of life. She was certainly very desirable. He felt, rather than saw, the envious sideways looks of the surrounding company but he didn't want things to escalate. He instinctively knew he was out of his depth. To escort a girl home afterwards and enjoy a short, sweet snogging session with no commitments either way was one thing but Clare, lazily leaning back in her chair, her knee lightly but insistently pressing his thigh, was a different proposition entirely. He wondered, flattered as he felt, whether he could handle it.

The interval over, the band started up with a set of waltzes. Clare was a good dancer, hanging lightly on his shoulder as they progressed slowly down the floor. The space was now quite crowded with other couples and Sandy liked this for, although it precluded doing any clever bits, it did make the couples hug closer together and Clare needed no urging.

Any caution Sandy felt about what might or might not happen was completely blotted out by the third waltz. As Clare's hair brushed against

35

his forehead, blocking his line of vision, he felt intoxicated by her aura. A violet light beam crossed her shoulder as she stepped back into the 1-2-3 rhythm, not ahead of his body but waiting for his thighs to propel her along.

The waltz was designed for lovers. Its magic reigned supreme over the swaying couples. Like flotsam on a slow tide of sweet sounds, spell-bound couples floated round and round, hoping this moment would last forever. Intoxicated by the romantic mist of the ballroom, many a marriage proposal would be made on such a night as this, to flounder, years later, in the routine-blunted lives of the partners, surrounded by screeching infants and pennants of damp washing, hanging from such space as a small kitchen might supply.

They came into the corner of the hall and traversed it neatly with a three-point turn. Sandy thought he saw a flicker of recognition in Clare's eyes as they passed a motley group of spectators. Older ladies, waiting expectantly to be honoured if they were lucky, by some Brylcreem-smeared loner and, further back, a knot of sullen boys, staring vacantly at the dancers. Sandy wondered what fun they got out of an evening such as this.

It was the same in all dance halls. Similar groups of youths would cling together unable, or not daring, to try their luck on the floor. Perhaps it was a fear of their mates' ribaldry that held them back. Better not to risk being the butt of their sarcasm, just stay with the crowd, drink, crack jokes and stare at those more willing to make a fool of themselves. But the envy bit deep into their collective mood and the bravura of the chat could not hide the sterility of their attitude.

His own friends were nowhere in sight, which usually meant they were having a good time and would probably not emerge from the crowds until after the last dance and the cloakroom crush began. He wondered if Ken had struck lucky. He usually did, in an effortless way, which the others hadn't the confidence to expect. If there were any sly questions posed by the girls of their acquaintance, Ken was usually the subject of their interest. *'When was his birthday?'* for instance and *'How old is he?'*, *'Is he going steady?'* and so on. The others took it for granted as this pattern established itself very early on, when the boys were in their early teens.

It was Ken the hungry glances were aimed at but this caused

amusement rather than jealously. That was until Pat appeared on the scene and then Ken's charms were a very real threat. Just a few years back, some of the girls at St. Luke's had made a habit of following the boys after closing time. There was no doubt in any of their minds who the magnet was.

They had all made fun of the girls, who gained no respect at all by this behaviour. By now, Ken had got used to this kind of attention, even expected it but it had not made him conceited. He possessed a sense of humour which made him see everything as a light form of entertainment. Ken's easy manner was the glue that held the group together. Without even trying, he was a natural leader and all sensed this.

With a strident final chord, the band finished its set of waltzes and Clare lit up a Craven A. cigarette after offering the box to Sandy. He gently declined for, although he didn't mind others smoking, any desire he may have harboured in his younger years when it may have seemed like sweet forbidden fruit, had been quite killed by the chain smoking habit of his father.

He could never quite forget the stale, impregnated smell of the hallway, with the jackets, raincoats and scarves all carrying that pervasive odour. It clung to all who passed through, adding another dimension of dinginess in an already drab space. He thought how none of his friends smoked. Although they had never mentioned the subject, he suspected they had similar reasons for not following the habit of their parents.

Clare leaned back, taking long, deep draws, the smoke lifting in slow loops about her dark curls and Sandy felt the pleasure she received from this simple ritual.

After some casual conversation, he sensed she had become somewhat uneasy and wondered if he had not lived up to the image she had originally glimpsed of him and was now getting bored. They found themselves dancing the last waltz and she seemed to relax again.

'Can I see you home?' Sandy ventured, trying to sound casual about it.

'If you like,' she answered, in a manner that suggested no other reply was contemplated.

Long queues were beginning to form by the cloakrooms and they separated to join their respective lines. He noticed his friends were already making their way out, each in company with a girl but, before he could identify their partners, other groups had massed in the exit and they were lost from view.

He collected his gabardine raincoat and saw that Clare was just about to leave her counter fifteen yards away. He started towards her, when a deafening shout exploded in his left ear.

'Oi, pimples!' He half turned to find a face, boiled red with anger, thrusting into his own. 'You were after Clare, weren't cha? Pimple face.'

Before he had time to react, another shout from the front made him realise he was completely encircled. They belonged to the sullen group around the bar earlier, although his mind couldn't grasp this in the quickening pace of events.

'You thieving git. She's married to my brother! And you're getting married to my boot!' The venom in his voice was chilling. Any attempt to explain his innocence was made unnecessary by the sudden punch which landed on the side of his jaw, tearing his lower lip. He staggered sideways, to be arrested by a knee-blow to the stomach. This may have been fortunate, for the other swinging punches couldn't land effectively on his slumped form and glanced off his shoulders and neck. The faces of his assailants leered down, excited by the helplessness of his position. All escape was blocked off and he knew he could only shield his face as best he could from the clumsily aimed blows.

At this point three bystanders intervened and the gang of six rapidly dispersed into the crowd. Sandy struggled to understand the trauma of the last few minutes. The elder group, who had prevented a more serious beating, helped him to his feet.

'Have you a clean handkerchief?' one asked. 'They've cut your lip and it's making a nice mess of you shirt.'

As they spoke, he focused on the slowly accumulating spots of blood that splattered on the white of his shirt-front. He stopped the flow as best he could and began to compose himself. His friends had left minutes before the attack and he wondered what else he had to think about. *'Clare'*, it came to him as his thoughts gained control again. He looked over to where he had last seen her, ten minutes before but she was gone. He scanned the exit area but there was no sign of her. She had disappeared as if she were a mirage.

Without further event, he walked the fifteen minutes to his front door. It was ironic this had happened to him, the most passive of the group. Apart from Speedway, cricket and dancing, he had little passionate feelings about anything. He had never been in love, never been mixed up in any trouble before. He wasn't even angry at his assailants, who seemed to have some scanty excuse for their behaviour but he did feel anger towards Clare, who must have known the danger she was involving him in. She probably made for the door at the first sign of trouble, leaving him to find his own way out of a bad situation.

His main worry now was facing his father. He would certainly seek reasons why he didn't give a better account of himself, in spite of being so heavily outnumbered. Sandy decided to exaggerate the number of his attackers to twelve. He felt better after these thoughts, in spite of his battered lip and the congealed blood that stained his chin.

Through a second floor window, he heard the melodious voice of Kenneth McKellar singing from a radio show. *'There is a brotherhood of men'* and, once again, with more emphasis, *'there is a brotherhood of men!'*. He smiled wanly and turned his key in the lock. It could have been a lot worse.

The Sheet Music Stall

It was 8.30 in the morning and very cold. Beads of frost glinted on the pebble path ahead. Ken had twenty more yards to go before he pulled the stall clear of the lock-up and into Southwark Park Road.

Six days of the week it stood idle, until Saturday came, when together with many other barrows, it was trundled out, to serve the crowds surging through the market known as 'The Blue'. It began at the 'Blue Anchor' pub and ended at the 'Coleen Bawn', taking its name from the former.

Not as big as its neighbour in the Tower Bridge Road, it was, nevertheless, richly stocked with a variety of goods. Hodge's fish, Tilly's sweets, Sid's second-hand clothing and the cat meat stall all jostled for trade, in competition with the more established shops.

Ken's hands gripped tightly the cold metal shaft. It needed all his strength to move off, from a stationary position. Once the stall was in motion the problem was to stop it, for the slope of the alley caused a build-up of speed and the tiny iron wheels, out of all proportion to the shed-like bulk above, screamed in protest as he steered into the left-hand turn of the busy road ahead.

Ken worked for Beryl, the sheet music lady, sometimes known as 'Foxtrot Beryl'. She paid him five shillings a week to position her stall outside the bakers by 9.00 am and return it to the lock-up by 5.30. It wasn't much money for the effort but he was pleased to have it, particularly with St. Luke's camping trip to Devon coming up.

Today was a special day. Beryl had offered him £1.00 extra to mind the stall while she attended a medical appointment. He didn't want to do it but he had always been in some awe of Beryl. In a market full of characters, she was outstanding. She knew absolutely everything about popular music and surprisingly, even a smattering about jazz, his special passion.

Her stall had become a mecca for the young men and girls of the neighbourhood, eager to keep abreast of the latest hits. Ken wasn't sure he could deal with all this enthusiasm about music he really despised. How would he know what the latest Beverly Sisters hit was? Some clever-Dick was sure to ask and, as for Doris Day, yuk! Nevertheless, he wouldn't be letting Beryl down.

After ten minutes hard graft, he guided the stall into the kerb by the bakers. Sid was already there on his left, hanging shirts in neat rows. Although his stuff was all second-hand, Sid kept everything scrupulously clean and the effect of his stall was not that of a jumble sale. He was touching seventy and retained a dignity of bearing and civilised manner in greeting his regular customers. Ken was struck forcibly by this, contrasting his gentle restraint with the pushy salesmanship of the shops in the Whitechapel Road. Without even trying, he was one nature's gentlemen.

'I've got something for you,' Sid beckoned. From a carrier bag he produced a pile of 78 speed gramophone records. Glinting from the dusty cardboard covers were the old familiar labels, Parlophone, Columbia and HMV. They all looked very promising but Ken knew from many wasted hours searching, that for every hundred run-of-the-mill records, you would be lucky to find one good jazz number. Would he be lucky today?

Picking up the first one, he read:

Louis Armstrong's Hot 5 and, in smaller gilt print below, the title, 'Willie the Weeper'. This was indeed treasure and in good condition too! The two discs beneath were Duke Ellington's Orchestra, not strictly to his taste but he could swap them. The last three were Bix Beiderbeck, Bessie Smith and King Olivers Creole Jazz Band. He could hardly believe his eyes.

'These are OK,' he said in a matter of fact way, suppressing any sign of pleasure, even to Sid. 'I'll have them.' Inwardly, he was bursting for joy. The King Oliver disc he knew was quite rare.

Having performed his first task, he now had a few hours to spare before standing in for Beryl. Conveying his treasure home, he then spent a most pleasurable session, listening to the exquisite sounds released by his wind-up gramophone.

At twelve o'clock he returned to the market. With its front flap dropped down, the stall reminded him of and old-fashioned bathing hut. Beryl greeted him from within, her peroxide blond hair lighting up the interior. Whatever the season was she always wore the same outfit, a low-cut satin blouse, (today it was emerald in hue) with three strings of pearls. Her fingers on both hands were encircled by gold rings, tapering to nails decorated in a deep shade of violet. It was a highly artificial and vulgar effect but it worked. She was, after all, in a branch of show business.

Jumping into the waiting taxi, (she went everywhere this way), she yelled over her shoulder, 'It's all priced, except for the Mario Lanza's at the back, they're five shillings each - you'll be alright - see you later!'

No sooner has Ken occupied her seat, customers began to arrive. Two middle-aged ladies caught his attention.

'Have you got the latest Donald Peers number? You know! The one he sung on the radio last night.'

'By a babbling brook,' her friend chipped in.

Even he hadn't been able to blot out the sound of the best-selling record in ages and found the requested piece quite quickly. As he accepted their money, he couldn't help noticing one of them wore two overcoats.

Sid caught his eye. 'That was Lily Thompson that was, she sings like an angel, every Saturday night in 'The Lilliput'. Hullo! The circus is coming.' He followed Sid's gaze and spotted a party of young Teds approaching, three boys and three girls. Ken found the teddy-boy fashion quite amusing and even stylish when worn with a tightly knotted college tie. The trouble was, it soon became a uniform like any other.

'Eiirrr! You're not Beryl!' The first girl engaged his eye in a frank stare.

'He's not Ethel either,' laughed one of her escorts. He was tall with a shock of ginger hair. His gleaming white shirt front sported a collar that was starched and then pressed in such a way that the lapels flew upwards and outwards.

Stretching his arm behind, Ginger tugged at a sleeve. 'Ask him Shirl - ask im about Frankie Vaughan.' Shirl came forward, cheeks reddening slightly as she became the focus of attention. Ken took in the line of her perfect teeth. As she spoke, jet drop earrings danced and glistened. 'Beryl promised me - last week - she said she'd get the new Frankie Vaughan number - have you got it?'

'What's it called?' Ken asked but, before Shirl could reply, her two friends stole the show with a double act. Singing in mock tenor tones. *'There's an old piano and it plays a tune behind the Green Door!'* - the last being screeched in high falsetto - *'I just can't rest - till I find out what's behind the Green Door!'* The duo faded amidst riotous clapping from the boys.

'Aintcha-gonna-sing the last bit then?' Ginger urged. 'I can only give you five out of ten otherwise.'

'That's more than enough! Yeah! More than enough!' Chorused his mates.

'If you're so clever, you finish it! You'd make a funny Frankie Vaughan with your hair.' The duo tossed their heads defiantly, flicking the short pony-tails that sprouted behind upswept hairstyles.

'Well,' Shirl asked with some anxiety, 'have you got it or not?'

Ken stooped to search the lower shelves. 'She may have put it under the counter.'

'She better have, we're singing at St. Saviour's tonight and we don't know the last three lines.'

Ken recognised the name of the popular Catholic Social Centre at Tower Bridge Road. It always seemed a livelier place than his own club, St. Luke's.

Trawling through a pile at the back, he eventually found 'Green Door'. Shirl's eyes flashed warmly towards him, with a touch more than gratitude. Ken got the message! What a pity she had the goon squad with her, she really was quite a dish.

The duo came to the fore again, 'Have you got the Telephone Song?'

'You know, Theresa Brewers' new number.' In reply to Ken's puzzled look, the duo eagerly demonstrated, *'Put a nickel in the telephone to ring my baby's number - got that - Brrrp - Brrrp - Brrrp - Brrrp - busy line!'*

Ginger's mates interrupted the serious ritual of combing their hair to quip, 'Sorry, the line's out of order, press button B and your money will be returned.'

'Ooooh look! He's got dandruff, all over his collar!' The duo knew all there was to know in the battle of the words.

Ken was glad of the diversion, it gave him time to think of a suitable reply. 'I'm sorry but we should have it by next week.' He had no idea what the telephone record was but this neat face-save was swept aside by the boys' counter-attack, 'Erierrr! It's not dandruff stupid, you're seeing spots before your eyes. It's all that singing,' and they began to playfully slap each other.

In good spirits, the Teds moved off. Shirl had given him one last invite of a smile, top lip curling back to reveal those film star teeth. Maybe one day she would come back alone. If she did, he would ask her to come out, up West with him, away from the world of youth clubs. He knew he could release her and many more like her, from the stifling inherited attitudes of the vast army of parents. He would be their liberator. This would be his vocation in life.

The Old Amsterdam

Geoffrey was angry and in pain, angry with himself for not seeing the rusty wire, stretched two inches above the path. He had taken the short cut across the bomb site, between the corner shop and the brick water-tank, like hundreds of times before. Years earlier, they had caught tadpoles in the few remaining inches of water, a left over from the wartime emergency reserves. Geoffrey's solid weight had carried him forward and hard over. His toes had stayed behind him.

By evening his shoulder had swollen considerably, to the extent that his mother had insisted on accompanying him to St. Olave's Hospital for an X-ray. Later, as they walked through the pea-green corridors, rubber doors swished open and shut with a soft, phut, phut. Each junction was enhanced by a battery of directional signs and ward names. Many were called after shipping lines, Blue Star, Ellerman, Blue Anchor and Cunard wards, a recognition of the close presence of Surrey Docks and the fact that forty percent of the patients were dockers.

They reached the Casualty Department eventually, a square room with a secretary and desk in one corner. A nurse moved busily between the office space and an adjacent door which led through to subdivided inner sections. She wore what was meant to be a reassuring countenance, a fixed smile which would remain in place even if an earthquake should suddenly split the floor apart. A row of posters offered scant diversion, 'KEEP DEATH OFF THE ROAD', was the heading to a harrowing image of a veiled widow. Another appealed, 'HELP STAMP OUT VD'.

The nurse was then at their side. 'Hmmm, that looks nasty,' (smiling all the while as she touched and prodded), 'Doctor will probably want an X-ray. I'm afraid you will be waiting for quite a time.'

Geoffrey looked at those waiting ahead of him, only six in number but at any time a serious casualty might arrive, needing all the attention available.

Sitting in the front row, a motorcyclist splayed all over a chair, head bandaged crudely. Both knuckles were grazed raw. A young mother sat nearby with her infant in her arms. She hummed gently in an attempt to still the paroxysm of coughing that shook the tiny form but it didn't seem to be working. Next to her an older man waited, sitting upright and very still. Geoffrey noticed splinters of timber on his sleeves and speculated that he was probably a stevedore on the timber ships over the road.

A long period of blankness then ensued. The nurse disappeared for fifteen minutes and no new patients arrived. Geoffrey had read the posters for the fifth time and his mother was still fussing about whether she had switched the radio off, when the rubber doors pushed open again.

A thin elegant waif of a girl stood on the threshold, looking uncertainly ahead. Her face appeared to be covered with an angry rash. Glancing nervously about she caught Geoffrey's eye and moved to sit beside him but, before she could do so, the secretary had interrupted her. 'Can I have your particulars, dear?' As she regained the seat beside him, he noticed the marks on her face again. What he had taken to be a rash, was no less than a network of shallow scratches.

By degrees, her story came out.

'The Old Amsterdam' was a pub close by, on the road to the docks. It enjoyed a mixed reputation. For the sailors of the Baltic fleet, it was home-from-home and when the timber ships sailed in, the Saloon Bar was soon packed with the voices of many nationalities.

Russians, Finns, Swedes and Germans, some would bring a squeeze-box and the sounds of lively dances could be heard by passers-by.

Because of its cosmopolitan atmosphere, some outsiders occasionally dropped by, broadcasters in the overseas service of the BBC, anxious to brush up their language skills but, by far the largest and most troublesome group were the gaggle of good-time girls, clinging like leeches to the drunken sailors and milking as much of their savings as they could before the ships left port. Geoffrey had seen them often, spilling onto the pavement after closing time, dressed in cheap furs, haggling amongst themselves, before dragging off some oblivious seaman.

It transpired that the girl beside him, whose name she said was Lucy, had arranged to meet a friend in the bar. In an agitated state, she continued her story. 'He liked to hear the Scandinavians speaking naturally, so he could use it in his programmes... He's in the BBC working on Norse Folk Tales. I don't know what happened tonight. I waited and waited... he just didn't turn up!' Geoffrey's mother quickly jumped into the pause, 'It's a very rough pub - oh my goodness! You shouldn't go there dearie! None of us locals do. We give it a wide berth!'

Telling her story had calmed the girl down somewhat and she eagerly filled in the rest. 'I waited in the bar... It was very crowded... no room to sit... then a seaman came over... with a sherry... I'd never seen him before...he got very friendly and I didn't know what to do... without being rude... I moved towards the door but before I could get out, three girls jumped on me... taking their men they said. They sounded Scottish, yelling, punching, then they started clawing my face.' At this, she broke down in a flood of tears.

This outburst brought the secretary over. 'Would you like a cup of tea, dearie?' she said taking the practical approach. Emotional outbursts were everyday occurrences in her job. It made it less boring. 'Doctor will be seeing you soon, I think.'

Being so absorbed in her tale, Geoffrey hadn't realised he was next-but-one to be seen. He imagined the extreme discomfort of the girl's situation. The hostile looks of the other females, the utter isolation of those alone in strange places. The mutterings and leers of the drunks. To the seasoned brigade of camp-followers, how frail and easy a victim she presented. He could see it all so clearly.

Just then, these thoughts were interrupted by another arrival. A tall seaman stepped forward, blood streaming down his face from a head wound. He waved towards them and shouted a cry of recognition. As he advanced, Geoffrey searched his mind but could find no memory of the man.

In a flash of movement, Lucy jumped from her seat and threw herself into the newcomer's arms.

'Oh Lord! What has happened to you?'

'Not much I think, a little quarrel, on my searchings for you. So! The Cats found you first and now we are here together.' His English was near-perfect.

As they embraced, she half turned and, seeing the perplexed stares, sent back an embarrassed smile. Even as Geoffrey tried to grasp the turn of events, history moved on.

'Will you come through now please?' The nurse stood at his shoulder, smile unchanged. He passed by the couple and into the surgery. When he emerged much later, a new set of faces looked up vacantly.

Stacey

Stacey slowly edged his craft along the tier of moored empty barges waiting to be towed away before the tide turned. He truly loved his work.

It had not been easy to get his lighterman's apprenticeship. Although his grandfather had been fifty years on the river, his own father had not pursued this tradition. Stacey had never found out why. All attempts to discuss and wheedle out why he chose to work in a mundane job as a warehouseman, instead of enjoying the freedom of the riverside, with its fresh air and open space, had met with silence.

On Monday, Stacey might be in Surrey Docks to pick up a barge load of timber and by late afternoon he would have reached his destination at Canal Wharf Peckham, with the help of a tow.

There was no nine to five pattern of working hours, everything depended on the tide. Often, he reached his destination after the buses had stopped for the night and had to trudge miles home. Sometimes, an assignment would take him as far as Rochester on the Medway.

There was no doubt, being a lighterman had enriched his life, introducing him to people he would otherwise never have experienced. Seamen from the Cuban sugar boats at Silvertown, Norwegians from the Baltic fleet, sailing in with the timber trade and the grumpy foremen of numerous riverside wharves, anxious to see their cargo stored away before the onset of a sudden shower.

All these impressions made his week an exciting one, so much so that he didn't have a lot of time out for nights out with the boys. A high tide in the evening invariably meant he would need to cast off his craft from some wharf-side quay and be making way while the current was running in his favour. He was proud of his hard won skills, that just one man alone, could nudge and steer his barge such long distances. Like all lightermen, he knew the currents and the slack water like the back of his hand, his long apprenticeship had seen to that.

The free society of the riverside community had made Stacey an independent man but it had left him little time for dating the opposite sex. Spasmodic romances had usually fallen foul of his most unsociable working hours. He still remembered vividly, the scene thrown by his last girl, Janice.

They had been invited to her best friend's wedding. That same day, he had to pick up a barge-load of spices at the Millwall Docks and deliver it to Cinnamon Wharf near Tower Bridge. It was a smelly but easy assignment and he had calculated on being home by late midday, leaving ample time to clean up and escort Janice to the church by 3pm.

It should have been a piece of cake. He had left early, catching a train to Greenwich and walking under the Thames by way of the narrow pedestrian tunnel dockers called the 'Pipe', had arrived at the docks by 8 am. He soon found his barge, tied two craft out from an old rusting cargo ship of eight thousand tons. He had seen the 'Jalajivan' before but had never picked up cargo from her. She was nearly unloaded and lying high out of the water. Like lorries at a warehouse, barges also had to queue in turn to be loaded by the stevedore barge hands. These were top gangs stowing three hundred tons a day overside and Stacey didn't have anything but the utmost confidence in their ability to fill his craft to the hatches and allow him to edge his way through the tangle of small craft, into clear water where the tug would be waiting.

To a layman, it was beyond understanding how a craft could be guided through the jumble of Sailormen (barges powered by sail), half-loaded vessels and the myriad of attendant launches, all jostling around the great bulk of the 'Jalajivan'.

After thirty minutes had passed, the barge closest in had received its full consignment. The stevedores clambered onto the barge on front of Stacey's and waited for the loaded vessel to nudge clear away from the ship's hull. Stacey watched the elderly lighterman miraculously push and pull his load between two sailing barges. All this was done with hardly any visible effort, so skilled was the old boy. Stacey recognised him and yelled across, *'Any winners lately, Ned?'* but the answer was lost on the wind and Stacey moved his craft next-but-one to shipside.

The stevedores worked like maniacs. The steam winch pumped up and down, sending screams from the tautened hawser as the load took weight. Juddering out, it bounced the set of spices over the heads of the four barge hands, then lowered it, jerking angrily into the hold. There was none of the graceful subtlety of the crane drivers accurate plumbing.

The steam winch pulled the thick derrick backwards and forwards, up and down, with all the ceremony of a rhino tramping through a waterhole.

A crane could, in the hands of a good driver, land its load onto a space the size of a tea-towel, even working blind, as long as the topman gave clear signals. The derrick in comparison, was like a dinosaur, clumsy, dangerous but the only answer if the ship was moored too far out from the quay, or if all the cranes were otherwise engaged.

Stacey watched the stevedores with interest, they were a veteran team, all but one, a youth of twenty two. As was always the case, they worked in two pairs. A set would be about twelve bags in a sling and each pair just had time to toss the bags in neat tiers across the hold before the next set was hanging overhead waiting to be lowered. It was a point of honour that you never kept the crane waiting, so hardly ever did the winchman have to pause before lowering his load to receive in turn the empty rope sling of the previous set, which minutes before had strained under a half ton weight. Placed on the vacant hook it was quickly whisked over the ship's side and into the vast vault of the hold.

The ship's tally clerk had told him earlier that the barge in front was only taking half a load and this he calculated, would mean his own craft would be ready to move under plumb quite soon. Clouds of cinnamon dust drifted up from the activity before him and Stacey settled back to read his newspaper.

It was then that a living nightmare occurred. Something of which all dockers tell of and dread, although it was now less common than in former days. A high-pitched scream, frightful in its intensity, came directly from the barge in front. Three stevedores stood in frozen tableaux, staring in dumbstruck horror at their younger colleague. He was crouching in agony with his arms clutched close to his stomach, his face the colour of grey asbestos. The set of bags it seems, had not landed in the right position and the signal was given to take the weight prior to a more exact placing. In this instant of time, the younger man had managed to get his hand trapped between the bags and the tautening grasp of the sling.

He had been unable to remove his hand in time to miss the savage bite of the rope as the set lifted a foot or so, into the air.

For such a little movement, the consequences were terrible. It had cost him a finger.

Within minutes, a stretcher and blanket were lowered down and, firmly strapped in, he was hauled up and over the ship's side in the same manner as the bags of cinnamon just minutes before. Stacey watched in disbelief as the ambulance sped away. He had witnessed the one accident, that always crops up in numerous cafe conversations and he wished to God he hadn't. Morbid variations of such events would circulate around the Dockside cafes for years afterwards. *'Did you hear about Patsy last week? He lost a finger on the Russian boat'*, *'Yeah! Crushed between two logs, a terrible thing! He won't be playing cards for a bit!'*

All work stopped as inquiries were made about the circumstances of the accident and it was eleven o'clock before work began on his craft. By then he knew he had little chance of finishing before lunch and passing through the lock gates by one o'clock. His hopes of meeting Janice as he arranged time looked pretty slim.

At all costs, he had somehow to forewarn her of his delay, so that she could proceed without him. To phone her was out of the question, he knew her family, like his, did not possess one. The other possibility was to ring his younger brother Geoffrey. He worked at a saw-mill quite near to Janice and should be able to slip around with a message. The switchboard answered his call and the telephonist promised to do all she could to contact Geoffrey. It was all in the lap of the gods! What more could he do?

At the best of times Janice was highly strung and he knew what the marriage of her childhood friend meant to her. She had talked about nothing else for weeks. She would really blow her top at being let down, whatever the circumstances. Women are so unreasonable, he mused, they always expected things to go like clockwork.

Somehow, the message at the sawmill did not reach his brother and Janice was left unaware of the trauma of events that had so delayed her boyfriend. Three o'clock came and went and at three thirty, with still no sight of Stacey, she phoned for a taxi and just made the church in time to see her friend escorted by her father advance down the aisle.

Much later, the inevitable scene took place. No amount of explaining could placate her rage, as he tried in vain to narrate the course of events. Janice didn't want to know about torn fingers and ambulances. Her special day had been ruined. What's more. *'Everybody had noticed her late arrival'*. It was all so humiliating and so the tirade went on, until even Stacey's patience was exhausted.

He left in exasperation, Janice could stew in her own tantrums, he had done the best he could. Sometimes it just wasn't worth the effort. He decided it was over with Janice. She could find someone more long-suffering, if she could.

He felt free again, free to dawdle home in the evenings. Free to lay in the bath as long as he liked without having to rush out at seven to make the pictures on time.

Since he and Janice had parted, life had been a lot easier. He did miss her at first, or rather, he missed the warmth of having a girl's arm tenderly locked into his and also, the looks of admiration that used to dart their way.

There was however, an intriguing challenge which he could either pursue, or ignore. Geoffrey had mentioned some months ago, that a new girl had moved into the next street. There was no reason why he should think any more about it, except for an encounter which brought them together in most unusual circumstances.

It happened at the time of the great fog. In the first days, many people struggled to work as best they could, using buses that crawled along at walking pace, or tube trains, if they lucky enough to live near a connection. For most, though, it meant walking gingerly through the yellow-grey swathes, hoping their sense of direction would eventually get them through.

It was in these conditions that Stacey found himself walking from London Bridge to his home. Reporting for work was just a formality, as nothing was moving on the river. No lighterage company were going to risk using their fleet of vessels with such a limited field of vision. He started out by following the line of railway arches that looped away towards Rotherhithe, passing one or two less certain travellers on the way. On reaching the junction with Tower Bridge Road, he drew abreast of a young lady, who clearly was in some difficulties. This was not surprising, as the fog blanket revealed no recognisable landmarks to act as pointers. Relieved to find another, she inquired if he were going in her direction and the two continued along together.

It transpired that she had moved to Bermondsey from the suburbs quite

recently and her name was Pat. They chatted easily and were both astonished to discover they each lived in the next street. Pat went on to explain that she had no friends at all in London, so didn't go out as much as she would like to, adding, 'I particularly want to sail under Tower Bridge, since a child, I've always wanted to do that.' Pat's wishes couldn't have fallen on better ears.

'I've a launch,' he remembered saying. 'I could take you one Sunday.' Stacey had the use of a small but sturdily powered boat, that he shared with three other lightermen. It was a necessary part of their transport but they all took turns to entertain friends and family with trips up and down the river on Sundays.

By the time they were almost at their homes, something had happened between them. An attraction existed, which in the space of a fifteen minute walk, was stronger than Stacey had experienced before. He instinctively knew she felt the same. They had come together almost in a predestined way, it seemed to justify all the unlikely plots of numerous films he had chuckled at. Both Pat and he were aware of the imminent consequences of this encounter. If they did come together again, Stacey thought it might be for good.

'I'll drop a note through your door when I've got the boat again,' he said and they waved farewell.

Two weeks later, Stacey faced Pat's door. The letter in his hand contained his best effort in writing for some years, indeed his only effort, apart from bills.

'Well, this is it,' he thought, as the envelope silently fell to the hall floor. Pat discreetly allowed her bedroom curtain to fall back into its private posture. She had seen enough, all that she wanted. Racing downstairs, her spirit soared. At last she was beginning to like London.

The Leader

Miss Cuthbertson was extremely popular as the youth leader of St. Luke's Club. She came from quite another world. Her thin, intense figure, dominated by an aristocratic hooked nose and humorous eyes. suggested a lively, self-sufficient personality and a born leader. She belonged to a select band, quite common in the 1920's and 1930's but now an almost extinct breed, that of the single travelling Englishwoman abroad.

At the age of twenty three, she had accepted the invitation of an aunt in Alexandria and, using this as her base, had traversed the Middle East from the Red Sea to Algeria. Archeology became the pretext for an extended love affair with the desert races. Her small allowance enabled her to live modestly but well. Many friendships had blossomed within the Arab communities but the clouds of war were gathering. When Benito Mussolini invaded Ethiopia, the writing was on the wall.

Women of her inclination were willing to cross deserts by the arduous passage of the camel train and rivers on the most primitive of rafts but they were not prepared to be caught on the wrong side of the Mediterranean when war was inevitably declared. Together with parties of elderly archeologists and diplomats' children, she found herself boarding a large steamship bound for Tilbury. Crowded into every available space in the cabins and mess rooms were a large number of kindred spirits, smitten by the East and not at all looking forward to the Northern climate and the conventional way of life they had left behind. They need not have worried, the world was about to undergo one of its periodic upheavals and nothing would be the same again.

The steamship sailed without event through the straits if Gibraltar and arrived in the Thames estuary a week before the declaration. She had decided to stay with an aunt in London, while considering what she might do with herself. The quickening pace of events settled the question for her. In Alexandria, she had chugged about in a tiny Austin 7 and, as a qualified driver, her course seemed obvious. Without delay, she enlisted in the Ambulance Service and, by the time of the first air-raids, found herself steering a brand new vehicle, one of a dedicated team.

Her posting was to an unfamiliar part of London. The Bermondsey Medical Mission was set in the industrial heartlands of the south-east, amongst the jam factories, cold stores and chocolate manufacturers. Miss Cuthbertson had hardly had time to introduce herself, when the first bombs fell. The Luftwaffe had correctly pinpointed Bermondsey as the food store of London and intended to flatten as much of it as possible.

Life became an endless cycle of sirens, frenzied emergency dashes, past deep craters and burnt-out buses and the collapse into exhausted oblivion at the end of her shift. The return journey to her aunt at Putney became too dangerous to continue and most nights she slept in make-shift beds at the unit.

The daylight raids became night-raids as the war moved into a different phase. The closest she came to a personal disaster was the night a Dornier bomber, blazing from nose to tail, crossed her at a height of fifty feet and crashed into a factory at the end of the street. Flying glass and debris rained about the ambulance but she was able to reverse down a side road and away from the chaos.

It was amidst all this that she had fallen in love. He was a doctor in the casualty ward at Guy's Hospital, not particularly young or old but a comfortable sort of chap. Part of her routine was to convey the more serious cases to Guys and their meetings, in the course of duty, became quite frequent. A nodding acquaintance grew quickly into deep affection and Miss Cuthbertson found herself utterly fulfilled, perhaps for the first time in her life. For her, the war had brought intense happiness but it was not to last.

As the war entered its final year, the VII rockets were launched from sites in Holland and Belgium, to fall with devastating accuracy on the population of the city. Without warning a street would exist and then be obliterated in the space of a second. Her doctor was one of the twenty five killed when a rocket fell in the courtyard of his railway station. In a state of numb suspension, she worked extra hours, channelling the misery of bereavement into the positive act of saving lives, volunteering at every opportunity to be at the scene of the unexploded bomb or land mine.

Then it was all over. The craters were filled in and the streets echoed to the sound of returning evacuees. The markets were busy and the cinemas surrounded by hopeful queues. Life returned to a kind of normality. She had to admit, she had enjoyed the dangers of the last few years and now, with the reuniting of families back from the country and the return of the fighting forces to their homes, she felt cut off from it all.

Another face of London revealed itself, one that lay dormant until the fighting was over. Old clans were beginning to reform. The common bond of loyalty, which helped with the war, was fragmenting into hundreds of aggressive self-important groups, all eager for as much power as they could squeeze from an exhausted and bankrupt country. This was a London she did not know or like. She desperately wanted to help the brave reforms of the post-war government - but how? Hers had been an active life and any sort of post which entailed sitting at a desk cluttered with forms, or associated with politics, was not for her.

Then a letter arrived. It contained an interesting and unexpected offer. A new Youth Club was being formed in an area near the docks, loosely associated to and backed by Church of England funds. Would Miss Cuthbertson consider becoming its first youth leader? Using her energy and enthusiasm to guide the Club through its early years.

It was a gift from the Gods. She had been on the point of leaving London. Many of her friends in the Ambulance Service had already moved away and some had been killed in the final rocket attacks. Increasingly she had felt a sense of uselessness, belonging to no particular group, in the rapid pace of social change.

Here was role she could fulfil, with clear-cut goals. A mixture of physical and mental challenges that excited her imagination. She accepted the post immediately and moved into a cosy flat above the clubhouse three months later. St. Luke's, as it came to be known, occupied a large rambling Victorian house in the gothic style. Corridors wandered throughout, gloriously inefficient, honeycombed with rooms all shapes and sizes and ideally suited to its purpose.

The boys were the first to arrive, twenty five in the first week, followed by a dozen girls. Soon the rooms echoed to the muffled chink of colliding billiard balls and the sounds of dance music from the main room. Here girls would pair off to practise a new step, the boys hardly ever bothered but would turn up in the last half-hour to go through the motions of jiving. On a full night the Club vibrated with high spirits.

From the first week, Miss Cuthbertson had struck a popular note with the members. She seemed to be worlds away from life as they knew it, the harassed long days of their parents, the shouts and scolding of the classroom. They felt, rather than thought about it. She lived untrammelled by the petty restrictions that seemed to bind others. Girls began to confide things to her that couldn't be discussed at home. The boys enjoyed telling her tall stories, testing her credulity with tales about the doomed first attempt to launch a Club some months back.

'Guess what Miss? My brother was playing billiards in the old railway arches when something jogged his elbow and his cue tore the table. When he turned to hit whoever it was, a big cart horse was staring right at him. It had come from the stables next door.'

'Didn't the horse win the trophy that year?' Somebody yelled over his shoulder.

'Don't you call me a liar. It's the gospel truth Miss.'

Miss Cuthbertson loved the endless attempts by the boys to impress her. Scuffles occasionally broke out but were never serious. She soon recognised the signs of bluff and counter-bluff and acted quickly to diffuse scenes before they came too heated. St. Luke's had become her extended family, the energy and respect of its youth nourished her personality and she felt complete again.

In the light of her acknowledged popularity and qualities of leadership, she was somewhat surprised to hear from the Governors that she needed some support. A sports correspondent, Mr Ross, would be arriving shortly to take charge of the football and cricket activities and generally help out.

He came on a motorbike, Brylcreemed dark hair and a thin moustache, exuding an air of conceited confidence. There was nothing overtly in his manner she could object to and he would certainly be very useful on the summer camp to Devon - but something wasn't quite right about him.

This early intuitive feeling was borne out quite forcibly some weeks later when, through force of habit, she opened a drawer in a cabinet which had previously been hers but was now used by Mr Ross. Half hidden beneath some membership forms, a group of magazines lay. Aware, as she was of her mistake, she couldn't nevertheless resist the impulse to flick open the first pages. What she saw filled her with shock and revolt. Angrily, she slammed the drawer shut.

Of all the dedicated candidates who applied for the post, ex-students, nurses and others, the panel had opted for the supposed worldly glamour of Fleet Street in choosing Mr Ross and what he might bring to the Club. Nothing glamorous was contained in the magazines. The few photographs she glimpsed were sordid and criminal. Anyone remotely interested in these obscenities had no right to be involved with a youth club.

She decided to say nothing about her discovery for the time being but keep a very close watch on all that occurred at St. Luke's. Her mind, troubled by this unwelcome revelation, turned to the complex task of organising the summer camp, to be held this year by the River Axe, in Devon. It would be a damp location but more problematic was the anxious letter, waiting to be answered, from the goose farmer in the next field. Her pen began to scratch for words to assuage his concern.

The Council of War

There could be worse places to go than St. Luke's on a rainy night. The club had functioned well under Miss Cuthbertson's guidance and, when word got around that another was coming to share her post, there was some consternation. She had created for all, a friendly haven and in return they were fiercely loyal. There could only be one leader. Anyone else was superfluous.

Thus it was that Mr Ross arrived, a sports writer of some standing, to help cover such activities as football, billiards and table tennis. He had taken the post with the expectation that he would find, waiting to be licked into shape, a ragged but eager group of youngsters, the clay from which to build a dynamic team. To his dismay, football at the club was a non-starter, the boys just lacked the commitment. 'Too much Saturday-night-at-the-Palaise and not enough Sunday morning practice,' he chided. Very few were willing to gather in the rain sodden park after a night out and, what's more, be yelled at for their pains. For Mr Ross was turning out to be something of a tyrant.

At first, his caustic comments were taken with good humour, in the rough and tumble life of the club but, after some months, his sarcasm began to grate and the boys wished they were back under the sole command of Miss Cuthbertson, with her free and easy manner.

If football was low on the boys' priorities, it was a different matter with table tennis. The club had gained a strong reputation as a nursery for talented players and had twice reached the semi-finals of the All-London Youth League. Three years previous, the Allison twins had won the doubles cup and this had fuelled the enthusiasm of the others.

Ken, Sandy and John could play reasonably well, devoting all of Wednesday night to practising backhand and forward drives but it was Geoffrey who held the club's attention. From the age of ten, he had shown remarkable powers of concentration in the game. However brilliant the opponent's strokes were, Geoffrey's relentless pressure would eventually wear them down. His friends often watched spellbound as he managed to retrieve a forehand smash, frequently below the table line, to the amazement of the other player, who had hit the ball with all his force.

Geoffrey was the only contender for the league cup, who would have any fighting chance of winning and, most nights, he was polishing up his attacking strokes. His playing was strengthened by the sudden arrival at the club of another adult. Occasionally, undergraduates from Oxford, or Cambridge would stay in the mission house nearby and play an active role in the club's programme. It relieved the tedium of study and also introduced them to a strata of society they had never encountered before.

Andy had arrived in Bermondsey after living most of his life in the Cotswolds. He was halfway through his medical studies at nearby Guy's Hospital and a night at the youth club was a welcome relief to the lectures on tropical diseases and the problems of the nervous system.

He immediately struck up a rapport with its members. The direct manner of the youngsters, he found quite refreshing. In spite of the disadvantages of education and environment, they faced the world with a radiant optimism. It had been quite a culture shock at first but now he warmed to the vitality of the community around him and returned less often to the tranquillity of the Cotswolds.

Like Geoffrey, he had spent much of his youth playing 'ping pong', as they called it, at the boarding school. It was hardly anything to boast about but he had been school champion for two years. This seemed to be the one bright memory of the austere establishment he was enclosed in for so long. How free these Bermondsey boys are, he contemplated, on his first visit to St. Luke's. An instant bond between Geoffrey and Andy was formed, when to his astonishment Andy lost by three points in a hard fought battle together. He wanted, just once to win a game with Geoffrey but the more matches they played together, the more remote this possibility seemed.

After a really gruelling day around the wards at Guys, he found himself in the evening at St. Luke's, smashing a ball across the table with great abandon, driving it from one side to the other and causing Geoffrey to leap about in agile but desperate defence. For once, Andy was on top of the game and really enjoying himself.

It was in this session that Mr Ross stopped by to watch.

'I've got a bigger bat if you need one,' he sniggered, as Geoffrey just failed to reach a ball that clipped the edge of the table. His cutting remark did not acknowledge the dozen or so shots Geoffrey had returned brilliantly minutes before. Neither player answered but played on in silence. Andy saw a gap in Geoffrey's defence and, bringing his bat from below his left hip, executed a fine backhand drive, his arm forging an arabesque in space. It was a classic shot, hurling high past his opponent's ear. Even so, impossible as it seemed, Geoffrey spun round and shooting his bat out, hit the ball blindly over his shoulder. It looped high over the net, to fall six inches short of the opposite end. Andy, who thought for one second the ball might just strike the table, sighed with relief and acknowledged Geoffrey's heroic attempt with: 'Hard luck! You only just missed!'.

By now, drawn by the tension, a little crowd had gathered to watch the match.

'We ought to get a higher ceiling for players like you,' Mr Ross commented, in caustic reference to the twelve foot high passage of Geoffrey's return stroke. Two of the younger girls sniggered and Geoffrey felt his cheeks turning red. Having scored a cheap laugh, Mr Ross left the assembly beaming.

Geoffrey played on half-heartedly, losing three points in a row. He was pleased when Andy made the winning shot and the game ended 21-16, the first match he had lost in six months.

'It must be my lucky night,' said Andy. He had been angered by the insensitive remarks of Mr Ross and the calculated manner in which they were expressed. What would motivate him to be so sarcastic? He pondered as he laid down his bat and walked away to the billiards room.

Two boys slouched lethargically in the background, as another steadied his cue with great deliberation. A cigarette lay on the table edge, its ash dropping to the green baize below. Try as he might, Andy couldn't find any interest in billiards at all. He knew most of the other youngsters regarded it as a an old man's sport. With this he was inclined to agree. It was all so very private, he felt he had intruded on their company. A confidentiality shared only by the players, so unlike the mood of the previous room. Silently, he closed the door and moved on.

The following evening, the boys met at the Empire Cafe. It was to be something of a war council. John had called the meeting. He was not in the slightest interested in football. It was quite wasted on him that his cousin, as centre forward for Millwall, was something of a local hero.

Mr Ross, as correspondent for the local Gazette, had devoted four paragraphs to pouring scorn on cousin Billy's performance this season. Many supporters, friends and John's wider family circle, were outraged by the personal and wholly unjustified attack. He had scored in every match so far, playing vigorous attacking football, he was as perplexed as his supporters, at the virulent nature of the article and had decided to ignore it.

His family had other ideas and, as it was known Mr Ross visited John's club in the evenings, John found himself being questioned closely on the nature of the youth leader. *'Was he an alcoholic?'* in which case he could have been under the influence, when he put pen to paper. John had to assure them that to his knowledge, his drinking habits were quite normal but he needed to talk about the incident with his friends.

Ken chewed stolidly on his sausage roll, stopping to remark, 'He's just a nasty piece of work - he enjoys winding people up.'

'Yeah. I wouldn't mind if there were any truth in it. Look at what he said to Donovan last Sunday. He let one goal in and Ross yelled out *'Go home and grow potatoes!'*. His girlfriend nearly killed him.'

'She's big enough,' Geoffrey quipped to Sandy's comment.

'My family want to do something about it, I dunno what.' John said, 'I don't think he could be sued, sports writers always exaggerate, the public are used to it.'

With that they fell silent. There seemed little they could do to teach him a lesson. He would continue to pour scorn on those whose faces he didn't like (and Geoffrey's was one of them) and also get away with unwarranted insults in the press.

'Is he coming on the camping trip to Devon?' Ken suddenly asked.

'Yes, for the whole two weeks, Miss Cuthbertson's only coming for the first week,' Sandy answered.

'That's it!' Geoffrey exclaimed, 'Let's stuff his sleeping bag full of spiders!'

'What about cow dung instead, we are next to a farm. Better still, make it both,' Ken laughed.

Feeling inspired, Geoffrey yelled across to the counter 'Another bacon sandwich, please May.' Plotting revenge was exacting work.

'There's other ways we can sort him out.'

'Yes but it's got to be at the camp.' On this they all agreed.

The meeting had accomplished something. A strategy was beginning to suggest itself, a series of plans, however slight, that could be developed, closer to the time.

Cheerfully, they left the Empire Cafe, with its smell of fatty bacon and the scent of spices impregnating the clothes of the other diners. Home they marched, under the railway arch, making its damp curving walls echo to their song.

'Wake up Millwall,
Can't play football,
Oh yes, we can,
We beat West Ham.'

Exeter Crown Court

The train pulled out of Waterloo Station and headed westwards. As it settled into a cosy rhythm, Geoffrey and Stacey stared out at the unfamiliar tapestry of fields and villages rushing by. It would be five hours before they reached Exeter and both had plenty of time to dwell on the events leading up to their journey.

It was fortunate that Geoffrey's summons to appear at Exeter Crown Court had come at a time when the Thames was in its slack period, between the summer timber trade and the busy pre-Christmas cargoes of fruits and nuts. It had not been difficult for Stacey to take a few days off to accompany his younger brother, not that he had asked him to but, as nobody in the family had ever been inside a court before, they all thought it best that Geoffrey should have some support. He knew most of what had actually happened at the Camp for, although his brother had been too embarrassed to mention more than the general events to his parents, to Stacey he had painted the full picture and it was clear that his evidence was vital for the prosecution case. It had all happened like this.

The day after the debacle of the collapsing tents, a constable was dispatched to enquire what all the noise was about. It so happened it was Geoffrey's turn to do camp duty that day, with a routine of peeling potatoes, carrots and parsnips occupying several hours. Usually there were two boys on duty but Geoffrey's partner had spent most of the morning collecting vital medicines.

So it was that only Mr Ross, the leader, and Geoffrey were in camp before lunch, except for the two village boys who sometimes helped Mr Ross. They had arrived early and disappeared from view towards the main tent. At 11am - and Geoffrey was sure of this because of the church clock chimes - a policeman appeared. Wheeling his bike before him he asked to be directed to the camp leader and Geoffrey, happy for a break in his boring fatigues, led the way to Mr Ross's tent.

As they came within a few yards, the sounds of grunts and tittering could be heard from the interior, suggesting the presence of more than one occupant. Without ceremony, the constable drew back the entrance flap to reveal a scene which at once both shocked and confused them. On a straw pallet the two village boys and Mr Ross were sprawled half naked. By a camp table stood three glasses of a yellowish liquid which could have come from any of the numerous bottles nearby.

While Geoffrey was still trying to understand the scene before him, the constable had no doubt what his next action should be.

'We were just having a lecture in first aid,' garbled the leader, hastily pulling up his trousers.

'Yes, so it looks like! You boys had better come with me and you had better come too.' The constable meticulously recorded Geoffrey's London address and intimated he would be needed as a witness. Then, with no further exchanges, the group of two boys and two adults trudged over the field to the lane and were lost in the shadows.

Geoffrey could form no clear attitude to what they had just witnessed, so far was it beyond his realm of experience. He returned back to the waiting heap of potatoes and began to peel.

On the campers return to London and St. Luke's, rumour after rumour circulated throughout the club. Some said Mr Ross had jumped bail and fled to North Africa. Others swore they had seen him at Millwall football ground but, wherever he was, he didn't dare show his face at the club again.

Finally the official-looking letter arrived, necessitating their present journey. As the train pulled into Exeter Station, Stacey ruminated on his own teenage years, quietly congratulating himself that he was always too busy to join a youth club. How would his old gang have handled the situation he wondered but he knew the answer to that one.

Like countless other trials, the case against Mr Ross was an anti-climax. Faced with the certainty of a prison sentence, Ross had indeed jumped bail. The judge ordered his detainment at the first opportunity and the case was adjourned. Both brothers were politely thanked for their attendance and given all due expenses. For the time being, it was over.

Stacey would have liked to visit the docks at Exeter. At least he could have impressed the other lightermen with details of the shipping operations but, instead, they chose to catch the next train back to Waterloo. His forthcoming wedding, problematic as it might be, was more rewarding to think about than the events of the last twelve hours. He settled comfortably back in his seat and began to tot up the number of guests on a scrap of paper.

For most of the train journey, Geoffrey kept his thoughts to himself, silently staring at the passing landscape. In spite of the adjournment, he was not disappointed with his day. The grandeur of the court, its weird figures in wigs and gowns and the little assemblies of people, tensely huddled together in corridors - it was the stuff of the cinema. But what a muddle it all was.

How could something so outwardly impressive creak along so slowly? Surely things could be done in a better way? What with all the hold-ups, Geoffrey had never drunk so much tea in all his life and they had only been in court a short while. The system seemed designed to waste the maximum amount of time and he was glad to be out of it.

In the not too distant future, there was a strong possibility that Geoffrey would have further opportunity to study court procedure. He would still find the same old muddle.

Tent Trouble

The rain drummed dully against the windows of the number one bus as it crawled in heavy traffic along Tower Bridge Road. Its lethargic passage exactly reflected Geoffrey's state of mind as he gazed idly at the girl sitting two seats in front and diagonally opposite. He knew her of course, almost every boy in the district did. It was all part of their troubled past together. Kathy was a pick-up at a local dance and lived in a Prefab on the other side of the market.

It was nine months since their parting but he still remembered the warm glow of their first weeks together, the cosy pattern of cinemas on Wednesdays and dancing on Friday and Saturday nights.

Her parents were quite unique, in so far as they were the only people he knew who owned a television set and very generous they were with it, inviting not only him but also his friends to view on special nights. On these occasions Kathy liked to preside over the company giving detailed information on what this or that series was about and who were the funniest comedians.

Their romance seemed to be going splendidly but odd things about her behaviour really puzzled him. Frequently when travelling home by bus after a late night out, Kathy often ducked down low in the seat or suddenly pulled up her scarf as if to hide her face. Her explanations were that she didn't want to be recognised by a particular passing youth or, as it happened, a whole gang of them.

At first, this was amusing but, as the weeks went by, this pattern intensified and Geoffrey's amusement turned to exasperation and finally to downright suspicion. He wondered if these encounters were truly 'past affairs', as she maintained, or old flames still burning brightly.

Finally, Kathy became increasingly difficult to contact. When he phoned, she was either at her sister's or washing her hair. It was clear he was being given the brush off. Calling at her Prefab to sort things out, her father mumbled sheepishly 'she was out for the evening'.

Geoffrey had to cut his losses. He was not one to dwell on such things and, after a few weeks, the trauma of the ensuing court case took his mind off their broken affair.

So much had happened in the last nine months - the Devon Camp, the sudden announcement of brother Stacey's engagement to Pat, his appearance as witness at Exeter Crown Court - that the closer he came to his call-up date for National Service, the faster life seemed to go. Because of his anxiety with court procedure, Stacey had travelled with him to Exeter and for that he was grateful, knowing how busy his brother and Pat were with their forthcoming wedding.

This was something he had yet to come to terms with. To think that Pat was to be his sister-in-law left him with mixed feelings, for only last year Pat was their 'golden girl', accompanying the boys to football and cricket matches and the other special treats. To a greater or lesser extent they were all in love with her but she maintained a delicate balance, part sister, part fantasy figure and always just out of reach.

Subconsciously, they knew it was better this way and it worked well until Stacey dropped his bombshell. Recalling the circumstances of how the two had met, their father declared with some truth, 'It's the only time I've known a fog to do any good'.

The bus rambled on past the Jam Factory and turned left at he traffic lights. The shape that was Kathy rose up and stood ready to alight. They exchanged a short frank glance together but no word of greeting was spoken and that would be the last they would see of each other.

Geoffrey felt no regrets he had lost her, this chance meeting confirmed it. As Kathy's form dissolved into the murk beyond, his thoughts turned to the dramatic events of the Summer Camp.

He would always remember it, for two separate events. One, a joyously high-spirited night of horse-play and the other, a sordid, wretched affair best forgotten.

Miss Cuthbertson had only stayed the first week as leader of the Camp, leaving Mr Ross in charge for the remainder of their stay. On the first night of her departure, all hell broke loose. A faint smile lightened Geoffrey's countenance as cinematic images flickered through his mind of that cold, damp evening.

It all began when the boys in the next tent decided to liven things up a bit. Sandy was almost asleep when he heard a rustling at the door-flap. Thinking it was cow from the next field, he quickly woke the others. Simultaneously, two arms broke through the flap and struggled frantically to release the fastenings. A fierce chorus of yelling from outside left them in no doubt now that their space was under heavy attack.

Arming themselves with any implements to hand, cricket stumps, heavy boots, mallets, they lashed out at the depressions buckling the canvas sides as the assailants tried equally hard to gain entrance. After ten minutes of thumping and bashing, Geoffrey, Ken, Sandy and the other three were still in possession of the tent and the boys outside withdrew to their own shelter, leaving behind a mess of churned up turf and an uneasy silence. Throughout the battle, neither side had seen the faces of their opponents, which made it all the more bizarre.

Fearing another attack they dare not go to sleep. Twenty minutes later the second assault began. Screams and yells echoed over the fields as they fought to beat off the raiders. In spite of their strong defence, one boy managed to wriggle under the canvas base and, leaping to the centre, tightly grasped the main pole. Sandy grabbed his waist and both fell to the ground, taking the tent pole with them. Deprived of all means of support the large circle of canvas above collapsed, burying them all under what, to a passing spectator, might have resembled a giant squashed mushroom.

For Geoffrey's side, the battle was clearly lost but the triumphant shouts of their opponents were silenced as they glanced towards their own tent. In the confusion of the moment, Ken had seen the unguarded shelter just ten yards away. Making a dash for it, he entered unchallenged. Quickly uprooting the centre-pole he brought the whole structure crashing to the ground.

Where two canvas silhouettes had stood less than an hour before, only a blank space now remained. The battle was a draw, one all.

Geoffrey remembered clearly that everyone involved was so exhausted, the task of re-erecting both shelters in the middle of the night just wasn't on. Instead, all slept under their respective flattened canvases, with heads at the perimeter and feet, like cheeses, pointing to the centre.

Geoffrey awoke to an unfamiliar sound. Standing just two feet from his head stood a duck inspecting the scene with slow deliberation. As he listened to its throaty murmurings he became aware of the heavy dew damping his hair, clothes and canvas alike.

But the duck wasn't the only creature to be unsettled by the melee of the previous night. By the lane traversing the campsite lay the New Bungalow Estate, the residents of which had not acquired homes in rural surroundings to be assaulted by the screams of Bermondsey scruffs! Indeed, even as the boys prepared breakfast, the phones were already ringing and the local duty Police Sergeant took the first of a series of angry complaints.

At that point a ringing sound with a different note interrupted Geoffrey's reverie. Focusing on the present, he took in the passenger about to alight and saw that he had reached his stop. Leaping to the exit he just managed to jump off as the bus sped on to Surrey Docks and the hinterland of Deptford beyond.

The Landslip

In spite of the sordid finale to the Devon trip, all at St. Luke's agreed it had been a great success. The boys had returned to London with faces polished by the western winds and glowing with vitality. Somewhat unusually on a venture such as this there were no broken bones, snake bites or appendicitis cases to report.

To Sandy, the Axe valley had been a revelation. He had never been to the Devon coast before, nor had any of them for that matter. Back in London he regretted the shortness of their stay and felt cheated of the many things they might have seen had their time not been curtailed by the arrest of Mr Ross.

One of his camp duties had been to collect the groceries and this had resulted in a fortunate consequence. The store window was plastered with the usual notices, 'Record Players', 'Bicycles' and 'Pet Rabbits' for sale, when a cream card caught his attention. Written in violet ink in a delicate script, it said:

Bed and Breakfast
Seaton Town Centre
Comfortable rooms at modest prices.
APPLY ..... Mrs Anning.

With no plan in mind he copied the details down thinking it might be useful for his parents. They never seemed to get organised enough to have a holiday and this might just tempt them.

It wasn't that they didn't like holidays. They certainly needed one, rather it was more the responsibility of finding the right place. Neither his mother or father, wished to be put in the position of what might be a disastrous choice.

He would do it for them, it was worth a try! Pocketing his scribbled copy, he got on with the main reason for his visit.

'16 lbs of spuds, 10 lbs of carrots, the same of onions and four cabbages please.'

The order placed, Sandy made his way to the River Axe. It had become his favourite spot and he wished there was time to explore the grand cliffs that dipped in diagonal contours to the waters of the estuary.

They were not the chalk-white images of the holiday posters, covered as they appeared to be in a dense sub-tropical vegetation. A perpetual mantle of mist made distances hard to judge.

Sandy felt determined to return at the first opportunity and explore them to the full.

A month later, Ken sat in the Prefab garden. The apple tree his father had planted five years earlier was giving a modest amount of shade if he inclined low enough in his deck-chair but, relaxed as he appeared, he was thinking quite hard.

Sandy's suggestion that they should revisit the Axe Valley this summer and spend another week exploring was very tempting. As free agents they could wander where they liked without the constraints of the camping fraternity and its irksome pattern of 'duties'. He had muted the idea last night but the others hadn't been interested.

John felt it was too soon after leaving the place and Geoffrey mumbled in agreement. Maybe their real reason was lack of the ready cash but that was no problem to him.

His earnings from Beryl on the sheet music stall had kept his savings in good account. Ken decided he would see Sandy that evening and make a plan of action.

Six hours later, both sat staring at the scrap of paper Sandy had passed across the kitchen table. Miraculously, the details of Mrs Anning's rooms had survived its stay with the loose ends of string, cough drops, pen knife and other detritus that filled the linings of his pocket.

'It seems OK to me. Why don't you write to her tonight, we could go in late August couldn't we?' Sandy lost no time in getting the letter off and seven days later Mrs Anning replied confirming a booking for the last week in August. They had just four weeks to wait and much to think about.

Meanwhile, Ken had received another less welcome letter. It bore the official stamp 'HMS' and informed him that he had passed his National Service Medical A1 and was to report to an enrolment centre with the RAF in early October. About this he had no opinion whatsoever, except to get it over and done with. With luck he might be able to get abroad. The Far East particularly appealed to him and he would try hard for that. He didn't fancy the square-bashing bit from what he had heard but that only lasted six weeks. Hednesford in Staffordshire was to be his training camp, wherever that was? He had a vague notion it was somewhere past Birmingham but the furthest North he had ever been was Paddington. Ken decided he would make the most of his remaining time as a civilian and looked forward to the bonus of an extra holiday with Sandy.

The intervening weeks passed swiftly without event until the day of departure came. With no lists of 'necessary items' to prepare, it had all been so beautifully simple. In a light drizzle they made their way to Waterloo and joined the queue at the platform barrier. Around them flowed the ceaseless movement of those leaving the city and the animated voices of the new arrivals united with friends and families again. A squad of young conscripts, kitbags stuffed to breaking point formed up behind them. Minutes later, the guard opened the gate and forward they shuffled to board the train.

Surrey, Hampshire, Wiltshire, Somerset all whistled by to the lulling rhythm of metal on metal. Tickety-toc - tockety-tic - tickety-toc, so continuous that Ken and Sandy were the only travellers in their compartment to remain awake throughout the journey. Eventually the locomotive chugged into Seaton Station greeted by flights of screaming seagulls dipping and swerving in and out of the trailing steam clouds till the platform canopy hid them from view. They had arrived at last and Seaton looked good!

Mrs Anning's house was easily found, being one of a short terrace all with neat front gardens bordered by golden privet and box hedges.

Sandy's knock was answered by a fair complexioned girl, perhaps a little more than a year older than them. She introduced herself as Mary and waved them inside.

'Mother's out shopping but if you follow me I'll show you your room.'

Up four flights of stairs they climbed, taking in the ornate turning of the bannisters and the solid wood panelling of the side walls. This was quite a novelty, all this darkness, light years away from the clean lines of the Prefab interiors they had left that morning. Sandy was reminded of a Sherlock Holmes film he had seen recently where shafts of sunlight crossed a very similar staircase such as this. The only difference being, a body lay silent on the second landing.

She stopped by a door with the name 'William' printed on it and beckoned them enter.

'It used to be my brother's room but he's in the Navy now.' This went some way to explaining the uneasy blend of faded grandeur and a very modern display of neatly framed photographs of warships. Both were struck by the height of the two windows. They stretched from floor to ceiling and opened onto a pretty wrought iron balcony.

'Is it safe to stand on it?' Sandy asked, peering at the street below.

'Nobody's done that for years, not since my brother left for Hong Kong. I don't think you should chance it.'

His glance wandered from her to the elegant marble fireplace surmounted by a photo of a fireman. 'It's my dad, you'll meet him later.' She then departed leaving them to unpack. From the bottom of the stairwell her voice carried upwards, 'Do come down for a cup of tea later.'

For Ken and Sandy, unpacking was a five minute job. Small items in a drawer and large ones in the wardrobe and then it was time to accept the invitation. Following the sound of voices, they entered a basement kitchen.

Mary Anning was handing a mug to a seated figure of a man. His feet were lost in an enamel bowl of steaming water which he stirred occasionally by lifting one foot or the other.

'Sit down boys. Like some biscuits?' He waved them towards chairs on the other side of the table and continued bathing and drying his feet. He was not a big man but wiry in build with no spare fat. His features suggested a good natured soul, emphasised by the humorous line of his mouth. Mary brought them mugs of tea and a plate of biscuits.

'Dad had to go in the marsh up to his knees, a sheep got stuck in the mud.' She sat down to finish her fizzy orange.

Sandy had time to study her in detail. As one would expect, her complexion was cleaner than the London girls he knew, with virtually no make-up at all. In contrast to her father's dark waves, short honey-blond locks curled upwards in bubble-like formations. She was not beautiful but the wide spacing of her features made for an attractive face, suggesting a generous nature with no hint of slyness. Style was not something Sandy gave much thought to and he certainly didn't consciously analyse Mary but he felt instinctively drawn to the wholesome uncomplicated air she projected.

Sensing the right moment to sound out the local scene, Ken asked, 'Is there anything special on this week in town? I know we are too early for the carnival.'

'Not in Seaton but on Friday night there is a big dance at Axminster, everybody's going to it.' Mary answered with a strong hint of invitation. 'The only thing is, it doesn't finish until well after the buses have stopped running.'

'What do you do, walk back to Seaton?' Sandy knew it was at least seven miles away and no dance was worth that.

Mary laughed at the idea of all that walking. 'Not after dancing all night. There's a taxi service. Harry Slaughter, he drives backwards and forwards until everybody's brought home. You just have to wait your turn, that's all.'

'It sounds great fun, we will definitely go.' On this the boys were unanimous and with that they thanked their hosts and departed intending to spend the evening in town.

The next two days were pleasant ones exploring the beach and the wreck of a coaster blown ashore in the winter gales. About the town farmers passed by at a leisurely pace, all gaiters and bow legs. Fishermen too, swinging buckets of freshly caught mackerel. They were far from the screeching factory sirens, summoning workers to the daily grind of jam and chocolate biscuit making. Although they had walked the town before, Sandy felt he was seeing it for the first time.

Wednesday was to be Lyme Regis day. They would walk all seven miles over the cliff path known as 'The Landslip', taking sandwiches and drinks to keep them going. Many years ago a huge section of cliff had broken away from the mainland but instead of collapsing in great piles of rubble, it had slid towards the sea as one intact piece, leaving a chasm in between. Nobody knew how deep it was as the bottom couldn't be seen. Every kind of native tree and shrub grew in profusion. Over all hung thick loops of vine making it even more impenetrable. Deer, foxes, rabbits, badgers, here all found sanctuary undisturbed by man.

The boys began their ascent up the one and only route, a twisting path traversing the top of the spine. Sometimes it was blocked by a fallen trunk, or a deep puddle swarming with gnats. After fifteen minutes they came to a mound on the left. Infinitesimal movements disturbed its surface. At close quarters they observed many vivid green lizards scuttling unconcerned about the sides of the heap. Sandy wondered what natural enemies they might have.

Some two miles of steady rambling brought them to a derelict cottage. There they decided to rest for lunch. Lost in a world of rampant nature the building, despite its lack of a roof and windows, struck a familiar and welcome note. Such sights were everyday experiences for those whose boyhood days were spent in the London of the post-war years. The Blitzed terraces and fractured factories served them just as well as the swings and roundabouts of the municipal parks. What did the inhabitants do, Sandy pondered, when the calamity struck? Were they pitched into the abyss that split apart the soil of their back garden? Or did they huddle together inside and survive as the cottage miraculously did? Finishing the last of the sandwiches, they moved on.

Two hours later the path began to slope gently downwards and glimpses of the sea appeared for the first time as the foliage grew less dense. Clearing a thin coppice of hazel, the sea walls of Lyme Regis came into view, sparkling in the middle distance. Plodding wearily into town, they were at once rewarded by the sight of a small friendly cinema.

There was only one thing to do and who said it first doesn't matter.

'I don't care what's showing - *Popeye*, *Donald Duck*, *Bob Hope*, anything!
- but let's go in and put our feet up.'

Seconds later, a scene from 'Fantasia' flashed across the screen. Dinosaurs
lumbered from one water hole to another, collapsing from the heat and exhaustion.
Mountains collided, while every lake was sucked dry by the merciless sun.

The boys knew just how they must have felt, these monsters from the Pleistocene
age and, as a new world dawned, in unison they raised their king-size choc-ices
and with an exquisite first bite, saluted the coming of a new era.

A Time to Dance

Ken looked over the heads of the dancers to the stage at the end of the long hall. There, pink and blue lights played around the six musicians, flashing on trumpeter and clarinettist in turn as they followed through with solo after solo. The drummer was something else! Sitting stoney-faced like a figure from the Old Testament, his hands moved a bare six inches to stroke steel brushes on brass cymbals with a swish-swish, - swish-swish, - swish-swish, an endless mesmerising purr.

A vocalist in a powder-blue dress fronted the band and was just beginning her number.

'East of the sun and west of the moon,' belted out in a strong northern accent but Ken wasn't interested in the lyrics, he was too busy taking in the astonishing likeness to his favourite film-star, 'Betty Grable', no less. Whether she had contrived this similarity, like so many of her profession, was irrelevant. What mattered was the strength of the echo. They had only just arrived but already the dance was beginning to look a success.

That Friday evening Mary had introduced the boys to her friend Hazel and together they caught the six o'clock bus to Axminster. Hazel was the exact opposite to Mary, both in appearance and temperament. She had a touch of the gipsy, Ken thought and that stirred a deep but unrequited taste for the exotic in the opposite sex, long yearned for but never encountered.

Sandy was first onto the floor, in a flurry of quick-steps with Mary. She was a good dancer and since it was her only leisure activity, it was just as well. They moved swiftly down the hall and into a natural pivot chassé, turning the corner with a beautifully executed manoeuvre and into the straight, skimming slower couples in passing.

Ken and Hazel studied them with admiration until Ken said, 'I think we can do better than that.'

'I hope so,' Hazel laughed as they stepped into the moving mass.

If Sandy was a skilful dancer, Ken was an audacious one, taking it all rather like a sporting challenge. Understanding the basic movements quite well, he couldn't resist the temptation to 'pep-it-up'. Whether this was influenced by his passion for jazz, or was just a quirk of his temperament, it certainly put his partner into some very challenging moments.

Catching the last number of the set of three, they sped down the floor as if making up for the previous lost dances. All was going well until an exuberant progressive chassé was blocked by the generous forms of a slow-moving couple, lumbering along at a pace of their own. Ken was studying the Betty Grable look-a-like as they passed the stage and Hazel's warning came too late.

On impact, the slow couple were shunted to one side as the momentum of Ken and Hazel's stride took them on and beyond before either had time to apologise.

A little later, in the interval, Hazel asked, 'Is it true you live in a Prefab? Mary told me so.'

'Not likely! I live in a proper house with a chimney and a real roof that stays on without being tied down.' Sandy couldn't resist the chance to make fun at Ken's expense, but Ken's retort was sharp and deadly accurate.

'Yeah, without a bathroom and a refrigerator.'

Mary then joined the exchange. She had never seen a Prefab before and her ignorance was informed only by the numerous cartoons in the popular press. 'Is it true you can see the sky through the roof?'

For more times than he could remember Ken found himself defending his home. Although in fact there was a slight chink of sky showing in his bedroom ceiling, not one drop of rain had passed through, even in the heaviest downpour.

Fascinated as they were to hear his praise, the girls still seemed unconvinced.

'Well if you come up to London you can see for yourself.'

With that the topic was dropped and the band filed back onto the stage. Of course, Sandy secretly agreed with Ken. The Prefabs were an immense improvement on the back-to-back, two-up, two-down terraces, flattened by the blitz.

The band kicked off with a set of novelty dances, much to their disgust. In the middle of the first waltz, the compere stopped the music and squeaked into the microphone, 'All right boys, any of you wearing a check pattern of any sort, please leave the floor.'

A dozen or so dancers drifted away and the music commenced, only to be interrupted before it had hardly started again. 'All right ladies, we haven't forgotten you. Who's wearing a pink blouse then? Kindly leave the floor.'

And so it went on. A purge of striped ties and black shoes left only six couples dancing.

'This is the last hurdle, ladies and gentlemen. It's goodbye to anyone whose names begin with a J.'

Two couples departed and, calling over those remaining, the compere handed each a box of Turkish Delights.

'Thank goodness that's over.' Hazel expressed their common feelings about the 'novelty dances' which were strictly for kids. They were there for the serious business of showing off their latest steps and the close clinches of the slow numbers, if they were lucky enough to have a band that knew its stuff. As they snuggled into the last waltz, the lights dimmed one by one. It had been an enjoyable night with no punch-ups and years later they might remember it with affection but now came the pressing problem of getting back to Seaton.

Outside, the street was crowded with old Austins, motorcycles with side cars and swarms of push-bikes all making off into the night. By the curb a butcher's van filled up with a party of teenagers. Following Mary, they came across 'Harry Slaughter's Taxi Service', twenty yards along. Peering inside the large black vehicle, it was clearly overflowing with passengers. Anxiously, Mary addressed the boiler-suited figure in the driving seat.

'Harry, you'll come back for us, won't you?'

The boiler-suit left the wheel and surveyed their group. 'I'll do better than that luv. We can squeeze you lot in, you bet we can!'

The girl sitting closest to the door eagerly agreed to sit on her partner's lap and, defying all the laws of physics, they managed to squash in amongst the others. Mary sat on Sandy's lap and Hazel on Ken's and they certainly weren't complaining!

The taxi moved off slowly, then picked up speed as it left Axminster. The speedometer climbed to 60 miles per hour as they raced along the flat marshes of the Axe Valley. What with the heat and the scent of bodies, Nature also became a passenger. The pressure of hips rubbing against hips and thighs pressed tightly together was beginning to raise the temperature of all, amongst other things. As they rounded a bend, Mary was thrown to one side and Sandy found himself holding her breasts in a vain attempt to keep her steady. Mary smiled her appreciation. It was all a weird mixture of pleasure and pain.

As they climbed the steep hill to Musbury, Hazel took advantage of the darkness to push Ken's hand under her skirt. This didn't surprise him one bit as he had been expecting it. Their bodies flattened into a semi-diagonal position and the night hid all under its discreet curtain. A kind of stupor fell over the other travellers as each pursued their own agenda.

Catching a glimpse of moonlight on the River Axe, Ken realised they were almost home.

A few minutes later Harry Slaughter drew to a halt by the clock-tower and the occupants slowly began the process of disentangling themselves. For some, the journey had ended all too soon.

The following day they didn't see Mary until the evening. She had already left for work before they sat down to breakfast. Mrs Anning preferred the boys to come down later and it suited them fine. That way she could cook in two shifts and take her time about it.

'So you had a good time last night then,' she asked as she placed eggs on toast and switched off the oven. 'Mary said you all enjoyed it.'

The boys nodded in agreement and munched on with their cereals. What could they say? In every way, it had turned out unexpectedly well, to say the least. They were leaving for London tomorrow and Friday night was the highlight of a near-perfect week.

The rest of the day was spent doing nothing in particular. Buying presents for the family occupied a pleasant hour, followed by lunch on the beach, a feast of sausage rolls washed down with lemonade. A round of miniature golf on the cliff-top behind finished the afternoon nicely, leaving them plenty of time to pack before tea.

On entering the house they passed Mr Anning carrying a mysterious parcel downstairs.

'See you later, boys.'

It took Sandy precisely ten minutes to fill his suitcase and Ken two minutes less. They would not have many more weeks to be so cavalier in the treatment of their possessions. In three months time, under the sadistic eye of some corporal, they would learn that packing and the display of one's belongings was a way of life, a religion even in some camps.

At the tea-table they were astonished to see Mr Anning resplendent in a white shirt, blue polka-dot tie and black waistcoat. Exuding an air of suspense, he announced shortly, 'I've got a surprise for you after we've eaten. We'll say no more about it till then.'

Mary then joined the table, blushing a little as she returned their glances. Mrs Anning continued a flow of inconsequential local gossip but a quiet mood fell over the table. All were feeling a little sad that it was their last night together.

Sensing his moment, Mr Anning arose and strode to the sideboard. Retrieving the mysterious long package, he placed it before them and proceeded with exaggerated ceremony to remove its wrappings.

Before them, all polished and gleaming, lay a brand new bagatelle board. 'Isn't she a beauty?'

Sandy had had a smaller version some years back and he was the first to acknowledge, 'It's the best I've ever seen.'

Mr Anning glowed with pride. 'I thought we would play a game tonight and christen it, so to speak.'

Before he could continue, Hazel burst into the room. Looking distressed and out of breath, she blurted out, 'I can't stay more than twenty minutes, I promised my sister last week I would help her with her wedding dress and she's arranged for the dressmaker to come tonight.

I can't let her down now. I just wanted to say goodbye before you left for London.'

Ken felt his world beginning to collapse. They had made an arrangement to meet tonight but now her puzzling hesitation began to make sense. She had hoped to change plans with her sister but it was a forlorn wish. She was only too aware of that as they left the taxi. For Sandy, too, this unforeseen development had thwarted his designs for the evening. He had in mind an exploration of the flora on the cliff-top with Mary. It would have been a goodbye to remember but, like it or not, they were all stuck with an evening spent around the bagatelle board. To have refused Mr Anning his boyish fun was out of the question.

Ken left the group and stood with Hazel in the porch. In spite of the warmth of their embrace both knew it was unlikely they would see each other again. As he clumsily explained, he could be anywhere in four months time, Cyprus, Germany or even Hong-Kong.

'I don't suppose I'll get much leave in the first six months but I've got your address and I will write'

With one last kiss, Hazel pushed herself away and ran off into the night. Ken watched her fleeting form until it was no more, then retraced his steps to the parlour. It had all gone so terribly wrong.

What was it Sandy's dad was always saying? 'A holiday is a gamble with the odds stacked against you.'

Perhaps! but in future years they would spend a lot more money on holidays in fashionable places and experience none of the joys these last few days of liberation had given them.

They sat back in the comfort of the carriage as the train slowly moved off, skirting the road they had taxied along with such frenetic speed. Each pondered silently the nature of the trip. If only the Army hadn't claimed two years of their lives just when things were looking up. Sandy felt he might have stayed there, found a job perhaps. There were plenty of Army and RAF camps in the area ... who knows, he might even be posted to one of them. One way or another, he would come back, of that he was sure.

As the train's incessant rhythm lulled his senses, he fell into a light sleep dreaming of Sunderland Flying Boats landing in a field bordered by rows of haystacks. Holding a flag in each hand, he ran up and down expertly guiding each plane in turn until all had taxied to a standstill.

The Wedding

The record churned endlessly around. No sooner had the last bars of music faded, the pick-up arm swung forward in automatic, to drop the needle at the beginning again. It had been playing so for fifteen minutes and no-one moved to change it. *Unforgettable... That's what you are... Unforgettable... Though near or far... Like a song of love that clings to me...*

Sandy lay in a drunken daze, between the sofa and the hearth. Beside him in the deep pile of the carpet, lay a fair-haired girl, his junior by a couple of years. He clasped the small of her back and pressed his lips into hers. She responded by clinging tightly to his neck with one arm, while the other fumbled with his loosened tie.

This was his third time home on leave since being called up for National Service. He had been posted to Lytham St. Annes, an RAF Station on the Lancashire coast and, to his surprise, found himself enjoying service life. His work on the communication systems allowed plenty of free time between shifts and the motley mixture of colleagues he shared his days with, were a sight more fun than the men in the ball bearing factory he had left a year ago.

The invitation to the wedding was timely and he was able to adjust his seven days leave quite smoothly. The signals unit were a relaxed bunch, ready to help each other out when time off was urgently needed, an attitude Sandy couldn't help comparing with the envy and meanness of his London work mates.

He hadn't analysed his feelings on 'life in the Forces'. Somewhere in his subconscious was the attraction to a wider geographical mixture of personalities. 'Geordies', 'Glaswegians', boys from the Norfolk Broads and the Belfast shipyards, with accents he hadn't yet converted into accessible English. Somehow they all worked together, knowing they had to make the best of it for two years.

A strong tug on his tie, brought him into the present, to study the face just inches from his nose. He knew next to nothing about this girl, whose lips so greedily squashed his own. Her features were generous. A snub blob of a nose between high cheek bones, flushed with excitement and almond shaped grey-blue eyes. Mascara smudged from a lower lid and Sandy gently brushed it away.

This warm creature beside him, would she have been so friendly twelve months ago, when he wore his office-boy suit and grey flannels at the weekend? He was still coming to terms with the effect his changed status had on the opposite sex. Not that this was the case with Alice? (That's what he thought she said her name was). Whether he was at home, or at Lytham St. Annes, the effect was the same. Girls who would previously have given him the brush-off, now had more than enough time. He had changed his original plan to join the army and instead, to his father's disgust, chosen the RAF.

Being in the signals section meant wearing on his arms their intriguing insignia, the flashes of 'Forked Lightening'. It was the sign of highly specialised skills and carried with it a certain mystique.

Sandy's work was so important that on the several occasions he had been charged, once for long hair, the other for wearing battle dress without a hat, (on Waterloo Station, no less). Both charges had been quashed on the grounds of 'Priority to Duty'. This rare verdict gave him immense satisfaction.

A blur of movement by the record player caught his attention. '... and forever more... That's how you'll stay,' ... 'Brrrp...'. Geoffrey had broken the litany of love and put in its place an up-tempo set of numbers by Ted Heath's Band. He had also got leave from an army depot, to help with his brother's wedding.

When the boys first heard the news that Geoffrey's brother, Stacey, was to marry Pat, they were quite shocked. Something which should have been in their control was being taken away. All of them, in varying degrees, had fallen for Pat, who had entered their world like a lily in a bed of wild irises

Except for Ken, the others had no illusions of their chances of winning her. Contact for them had been no more than flirtatious doorstep conversations. Ken had managed a little better. She had accepted his invite to come rowing in Southwark Park but he hadn't been able to develop further this promising start. The others were secretly pleased at this. For once, Ken hadn't put them in the shade.

The boys were baffled as to how Stacey had met her. Geoffrey knew nothing of his brother's meeting in the fog with Pat. It was just as much a mystery to him as to the others. Now Pat was becoming his sister-in-law, he was delighted. As for the wider circle of the two families, they were still recovering from the speed of events. From first encounter, to that solemn moment before the priest, just six hours ago, only twelve months had elapsed.

On one thing all were agreed. As Pat and Stacey walked down the aisle, man and wife, it was clear they were made for each other. St. Joseph's, at Paradise Street had seen many handsome couples but Pat, in her bridal gown of silvery satin, appeared to move in a luminous cloud of reflected light and Stacey, in charcoal-grey suit, appeared taller than before. His tough presence, the perfect foil to Pat's vibrancy. It was a wedding all mums and dads, aunts and uncles could be proud of, a scene of simple dignified beauty, without gimmicks.

Pat's parents had staged a good buffet feast afterwards, giving the whole of the bottom floor to the occasion. Guests wandered from the parlour to the kitchen and into the pretty back garden. From the walnut upright piano, Uncle Bill thumped out a string of lively tunes. It was a curious fact that although the tempo changed from the quicksteps to waltzes, they all sounded extensions of the same melody. Aunt Mabel, an obscure relative of Pat's, sang loudly and certainly with passion. Sometimes, she even managed the same tune as the pianist, except that whole sections of the lyrics went missing, as her memory fought a losing battle with four glasses of sherry. Sporadic outbreaks of dancing continued throughout the evening, petering out as guests sank red-faced and thirsty onto the Davenport.

As the evening moved into the night, the younger group detached themselves from the main party and retired to Geoffrey's house nearby. It was all cleverly worked out in advance. As Geoffrey's parents were sure to be involved in the main event till midnight at least, it left the way clear for Geoffrey to stage his own do.

All his friends were there, except for John, who was away on a special weapons course. Ken had brought Sheila, his steady girlfriend now, although he was reluctant to admit it. Sandy had come by himself and was pleased to see that Sheila had invited some of her friends. In all, it was a cosy group, three boys and three girls, with something of the intrigue of the blind date about it.

On the latter, Sandy was something of an expert. His work in the Signal's Section had some unexpected bonuses, such as dealing with the large numbers of hopeful girls, telephonists in the main, all looking for a romantic date with an airman. At times, so many of these would ring through, the switchboard would be jammed, thus preventing official calls from leaving the camp. Only the promise of a blind date would persuade them to ring off and leave his lines free. Sometimes, he thought he was in the wrong business.

To aid him in this earthy task of matchmaking, he kept a book, with all the regular callers carefully detailed, such as: Alice, tall brunette, loves dancing and Londoners; Katie, plump redhead, enjoys going to the cinema. His biggest success had been with the camp cook and the telephonist from the waterboard. Four months after he had effected a meeting, they were about to get engaged. This meant special favours in return. There would always be a meal for Sandy, whatever the time of day. He had enlisted as a conscientious and rather conventional boy, to become a skilled manipulator of the system, a fixer!

For Ken, it had been much harder to make the wedding. He was based at RAF Kenley, an operational flying station and the best he could manage was a forty eight hour pass. Most weekends he could get home but the nature of his work, with a Radar unit, meant there was more likelihood of leave cancellation when various exercises were taking place.

Sandy had noticed a distinct personality change in Ken since their last meeting. He was far less conceited, perhaps the steadying influence of

Sheila was as much responsible as the discipline of the Air Force. Sandy would not have taken into account that his own growing assertiveness had levelled the playing field between them.

Sandy then felt the tug of Alice's trapped skirt, as she pulled free and sat up on her elbows. 'Can I have a glass of orange juice? I'm so dry.'

'OK, I'm pretty dry myself.'

With that, he heaved himself to his feet and walked unsteadily into the kitchen. On his return, he noticed a grey hump on the sofa, two forms, obscured by a blanket. From the lower hem, four feet appeared, two of these dangling a pair of white stilettos.

'Geoffrey's doing all right,' he muttered, handing Alice her drink.

'So are you,' she retorted and then, after a pause, 'will we see each other again?'

'Yes, I'd like that a lot but I won't be home again for a few months.'

'I'll wait, if you want me to.' The soft tenderness of her words would stay with him when he returned 'up North'. He felt grateful towards Sheila for bringing her friends, they had all done 'all right'.

'You promise me you'll wait?' he urged. In answer, Alice began vigorously kissing his neck.

A sudden loud crack from outside, disturbed the amorous scene and Geoffrey ran to the window. Dim yellow light from a street lamp revealed the strangest of sights. Over a privet bush and flat on his back, lay his father. The shrub had broken his fall, pitching him onto the garden and away from the hard path. He lay motionless, making no attempt to regain his feet. Geoffrey's mother was going through the motions of pulling him up but, even as he watched, she too lost her balance and fell on top of his father. Together they lay, incapable of any further effort.

'Quick! Give me a hand!' Geoffrey yelled and raced down the stairs to join his parents. Neither were hurt. As is often the case, those in a state of oblivion do not seem to suffer the cuts and bruises of those in a similar predicament but fully conscious. Not too steady themselves, the boys struggled first with one and then with the other, half pulling, half carrying them up the narrow stairs to their own bed. Geoffrey wiped twigs and patches of soil from his father's face and hands but both parents were past caring, being deep in the land of nod.

Sandy joined the others in the kitchen. The collapsing parents had quite taken the edge off the romantic mood and the right moment had come for a hot mug of tea. Over the rising steam, Sandy surveyed the others. A year in the Forces had seen the boys change, chrysalid-like, from cocky teenagers, to early manhood. Not so long ago, the last scene might have been played with reversed roles. Now it was they who were the protectors, the parents reverting to carefree juveniles, on this day of days and didn't they deserve to?

The recent past was looking more distant every month. The youth club days, the fairground fiasco, the arrest of the sports writer, all slipping far behind. Picking Alice's raincoat from the hook on the door, he settled it on her shoulders and softly urged, 'Shall we go?'

As they walked through the railway arches dripping with damp, it occurred to him how lucky Pat and Stacey were, of the distinct advantages of having a home of your own, to share things with someone. It might be Alice, it might be another but soon it would be sorted out.

That time was nearly here.